The Ego Effect

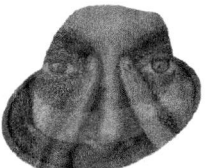

Creative Hats

First published in Great Britain, 2023 by Creative Hats Press, a division of Creative Hats.

First published in hardback in Hertfordshire in 2023 by Creative Hats Press, an imprint of Creative Hats.

This paperback edition published in 2023.

Copyright © Nicola Warner, 2023

The moral rights of Nicola Warner to be identified as authors of this work has been asserted by them in accordance with the © Copyright, Design and Patent Act, 1988.

This is a work of fiction. Names, characters, business, events and incidents are the products of the author's imagination. Any resemblance to actual persons, living or dead, or actual events is purely coincidental.

All rights reserved. No part of this publication may be reproduced, stored in a retrieval system, or transmitted in any form or by any means, electronic, mechanical, photocopying, recording or otherwise without the prior written permission of the publishers. This book may not be lent, hired out, resold, or otherwise disposed of by way of trade in any form of binding or cover other than that in which it is published, without the prior consent of the publishers.

Cover design by: C H Books

Edited by: Creative Hats

Also by Nicola Warner

Elephant in the Room
Fantastic Writers and Where to Read Them
Down the Inkwell

Dan Hayes Greatest Hits

1 - Chasing Dreams…………...………………. 2

2 - Haunted By You…....……………………... 10

3 - Mother Knows Best ….……………………. 17

4 - That's What Mothers Do…..…………….... 24

5 - Take Me Home…………………………... 34

6 - The After Effect….…………………………. 41

7 - Girl At The Bar...…………………………… 54

8 - Help Me Remember ..……………………... 59

9 - Dirty Laundry ...…………………………... 70

10 - Bottled Up Love…..……………………... 78

11 - Here Comes The Sun …………………… 91

12 - Therapy ………………………………….. 96

13 - Why Did You Go ……………………….. 104

14 - He Got What He Deserved..……………........ 125

15 - The Message Was Clear ………………… 135

16 - Let's Start This Again …………………… 144

17 - Am I Ready? …………………………….. 150

18 - The Day I Held You …………………….. 157

19 - How I Treated You …………………….. 165

20 - She's Mine……………………................. 172

21 - Many Happy Returns	176
22 - Cup Of Tea	189
23 - Sleepover	193
24 - Is This Love Real	196
25 - Never Enough	201
26 - Explain Yourselves	206
27 - Devil In The Detail	211
28 - Message In A Bottle	218
29 - It's A Little Bit Funny	224
30 - Rip It Off	236
31 - When The Lights Go Out	243
32 - No One Likes To Say Goodbye	247
33 - Writing Again	257
34 - Starting Over	263
35 - Back In Business	275
36 - Emilia	284

The Ego Effect

NICOLA WARNER

Creative Hats

Egotism (noun): the drive to maintain and/or enhance a favourable view of oneself and generally features an inflated opinion of one's personal features and importance distinguished by a person's amplified vision of self-importance. It often includes intellectual, physical, social, and other overestimations. The egotist has an overwhelming sense of the centrality of the 'me' regarding their personal qualities.

The questions which remain are:

Is an egotist created or born that way?

And/or capable of love?

The Ego Effect

01 – Chasing Dreams

Many people have no idea what career is for them, but Dan Hayes had been chasing dreams since he was 12 years old, driven by a hunger for fame and fortune. He longed to be recognised and he worked hard to perfect his performance. Music was always something he was passionate about; it was also his escape, and he was certain it was the career for him. He was told by his mother that as a baby his favourite toy was a small plastic yellow guitar, which he carried everywhere, although he didn't remember this himself, it would always be something he would use in interviews to show how much of an impact music had on him from a young age.

His older brother, Jed, also loved music, and although he had studied music it was never a passion to pursue a career as a performer. His passion was to write and produce the music for other artists to perform, and, of course, offered this to his younger brother. They would spend hours picking guitars and uploading audio clips onto their computer after school and on weekends.

The crowd roared, hysterical teenagers stretched their arms out, pleading with him to take notice. He felt an overwhelming power pulsate through him. Stood proud, glowing under the spotlight, proclaiming his undying love and gratitude to every one of them, thanking them for getting him where he was today. They screamed louder and louder, holding on to his every word.

This was it for him. This was home, where he belonged. He was the king of a loyal pride, who praised him for everything he had achieved. He shot a wink over to a couple of girls in the front row, who lost themselves in high-pitched screams. He smiled to himself, letting out a cheeky wince of laugh, as he teased them with the melody of the next song.

Dan moved across the stage constantly, never paying more attention to one side than the other. His pre-show nerves now overtaken with adrenaline; it spurred him to jump backwards off the front of a drum set. His drummer wasn't too impressed, despite how impressive it was. He landed, stumbled backwards, the guitarist to the side, steadied him. 'Nearly!' He joked to the crowd, 'it's a good job these guys have my back!' He patted his guitarist on the shoulder and presented another cheeky grin.

The crowd enjoyed the interaction he gave them, the rumbled cheers surfed through the crowd again, crashing an overwhelming wave of admiration. He welcomed it with open arms. Accepting their praise.

They hated the end of the show, and he always felt their disappointment as they pleaded with him for just one final song, he would oblige, of course and give them what they craved. The final encore would always be a firm favourite and one that carried a special place in his heart. It was the first song that he had not only written himself but was the first to reach number one in the charts. Of course, he had had other chart toppers, but most were either covers, or songs that were written for him. *This one was his*, he always bragged.

The lights went out. The chattering crowds echoed through the arena as his fans made their way to the exit. He made his way down the side steps to his allocated area backstage. As he walked past members of his team, he would be congratulated with a pat on the back, 'great show tonight', 'you were on fire', 'ready for the next one?' Dan smiled and thanked them as he wandered to his dressing room. He needed a cold drink and a shower, his clothes were soaked in sweat, even with intermittent costume changes. They were always rushed, and he would never have time to dry himself completely before having to return to the stage.

Dan collapsed into a small chair in front of a brightly lit mirror, his face red, breathing only just starting to return to normal and forehead still glistening with the aftermath of his performance. He opened the door to a small travel fridge and swiped a bottle of icy water then downed it to quench his thirst.

'Another great one!' Ruth praised.

Dan spun himself round in his chair towards the direction of his mother's voice, as she popped her head round the door.

'Let's see if you can better yourself tomorrow night!' she challenged him.

'No challenge there then,' he scoffed, as she disappeared down the hall. Dan's damp shirt now clung to him like a second layer of skin. He pulled it free over his head and jumped into the small cubicle which housed his shower.

Feeling somewhat refreshed, the shower was only good enough for running the sweat off his body, not nearly as powerful as the one at the hotel. Dan changed into fresh clothes and put his costumes on the side of the dresser ready to be cleaned for tomorrow's show.

'I hope you don't plan on bringing that with you!'

He turned to see his bandmate in the doorway and shot him a puzzled look. 'Well, I can't leave it here, I need to bring it back to the hotel,' Dan said as he swung his backpack over his shoulder.

'Ah well, you'll just have to leave it in the car ... we're going to a bar,' his bandmate announced. 'And don't worry, they serve food!'

Dan had just turned 15 years old, he knew that he would never be allowed in an over 18's bar, no matter who he claimed to be. He had tried to get into a London club once, telling Ruth that they were taking him out for pizza. It was a mission impossible with his celebrity status, the bouncers knew how old he was, and no offer of an autograph or photo was enough for them to turn a blind eye. Ruth seemed oblivious that he would come back to the hotel without his bandmates and still hungry. She'd greet him with a "did you have fun love?"

They headed out to the bar, accompanied by his mother, she wanted to be sure he was fed and back at a reasonable hour. He had more rehearsals the next day for yet another show. They were led to a long table in the middle of the restaurant, he sat down next to one of the band members and studied the menu, even though he already knew what he wanted. Burgers. Always burgers. Meanwhile his mother, studied the drinks menu, spoilt for choice, she decided on a vodka and coke with a side order of fries.

As he tucked into his burger he joined in with laughs as his band reminisced about performances. A glass slid into view, with a wink from his guitarist.

'Drink up mate!' they laughed.

Dan knew immediately by the mischievous twinkle in their eyes that this wasn't an ordinary glass of Coca-Cola. He glanced over to his mum at the bottom end of the table who was chatting happily with the waiter. He nodded a thank you at his bandmate and downed the concoction, hoping that the faster he drank it the less likely was to hit his tongue. But he could taste the sharp, bitter spirit that was hidden by the mixer. It hit the back of his throat hard, making his eyes water and stomach turn. Desperately not wanting to make a fool of himself he closed his eyes and forced it down with a loud gulp. He gasped for air and coughed, nearly inviting it back up.

'Are you okay love?' Ruth asked.

'Yea!' Dan spluttered, 'went down the wrong way!'

Dan's bandmates cheered. He received a pat on the back from those closest. 'Well done mate; we were sure you were going to be sick!' They laughed.

As each year passed, Dan grew in popularity. He quickly became aware that he could have or do anything he wanted. His songs were always a hit. Fans swarmed around him in public. He was caught in love triangles, sparking feuds between girls that had never met, and of course that kept him in the headlines. Scandals sell after all.

If people were talking about him, good or bad, he was happy, it meant he knew he was an interest, he was relevant. While he revelled in the attention of the headlines, his behaviour impacted those around him. Especially that of his mother, Ruth. His mum's health deteriorated, though she would never let that show. Her alcohol intake had more than doubled, sometimes she would hide a small metal flask in her bag, in case the need struck whilst she was out of range of a liquor bar.

His record company put a warning in writing, expressing their concerns over drug allegations, late night parties, this was not an image they wanted to support. He carelessly shrugged it off with devilish chuckles, 'they don't want to work with me, that's their loss. There are plenty of other labels out there that would take me on in a heartbeat, the fans love me, I bring in the money, you can't deny that!' His ego took the reins on most of his actions and that inevitably was his downfall.

02 – Haunted By You

Dan lay there, empty. The weight of his past pressing against his chest. The crowds that once echoed with praise and love haunting him; their ghostly whispers teased. He continued to stare at the blurred circle of the ceiling fan, spinning continuously out of control, much like his life, desperately clinging on to its fixings. He sighed and took another sip of his Jack Daniels and rested his head against the cushioned headboard of his double bed.

He spent a lot of time in his bedroom, it was filled with memorabilia from happier times. His first album went platinum, his plaque hung proudly on the wall opposite him. He thought that if it was the first thing he saw in the morning, it would bring inspiration for the day ahead. Now it's just a gleaming reminder of the life he once had. He stared at it blankly for a while, and almost considered taking it down.

He placed his empty glass on the bedside table and stumbled over to a mountain of clothes in the far corner of the room. He flung them behind him, scattering them in every direction until he unveiled the guitar buried underneath. He hesitated, *what are you doing? Pick up the damn guitar!* He lifted it from the stand and looked it over, it glistened like new. It felt familiar, like an old friend, and in a strange way it was comforting. He wandered back over to his bed and perched on the corner resting the body of the guitar on his legs. He sat and fiddled with the turning keys one by one plucking the strings along the way until each note was perfected.

Silence filled the room. He didn't play anything; he just held the guitar close to him. His guitar pick fell from his grasp and bounced silently onto the floor. He didn't pick it up, he couldn't, not even to play one of his songs. The memories attached to them were still too raw, even after all these years. The deflation of enthusiasm crippled him. *What's the point?* He got up and returned the guitar to its resting place. *Maybe another time.* He walked round the side of his bed and picked up the Jack Daniels bottle, emptying its contents into his glass, underestimating the amount the glass could hold. He picked up the overflowing glass, spilling half down his arm and threw the remains towards his mouth.

One day, I will get it all back, he told himself, 'You watch mate!' he slurred to his reflection in the mirror, 'We will get it all back! They *want* us! They *need* the music, baby!' He gave himself a "you got this" finger point and stumbled back onto the bed, leaning himself up against the headboard. Dan glared at his reflection through droopy eyes. He could hear the crowd faintly chanting his name, begging him for the final encore.

He squinted at the fiery glaze peering through a slight gap in the curtain, shooting his head away when the pain got too much. The smell of stale alcohol lay heavy in the atmosphere, hitting the back of his throat, and making his stomach turn. He was sure that whatever he could feel bubbling in his stomach would make its grand appearance the moment he stumbled to his feet. Groaning, he cradled his face, pulled the duvet up over his head, and took a deep breath.

The familiar sound of cupboard doors banging disturbed him, crockery clashing to its near death and muffled voices bouncing back and forth before turning silent. Heavy stomps made their way up the stairs, moving closer to his bedroom. The door flung open, with his mother still attached to the handle.

'Oh, good you're awake,' she said as she steadied her footing, 'come downstairs, breakfast is getting cold.'

He glared at her as she disappeared back down the hall. He rolled his eyes. Pushing the duvet down with his feet, he hopped out of bed and hurried down after her. He was greeted with the aroma of bacon, eggs, and a thin layer of smoke that was slowly filling the room. She always burnt the eggs. He sat down at the table alongside his father who was engrossed in the morning paper. Every so often his hand would appear from behind it, fumbling around for his coffee mug. His mother was still flustering round the stove, checking that everything was off before placing plates in front of them both.

'Are you not eating, Mum?' he asked.

'Oh, no, love, I have my coffee to keep me going,' she smiled as she cradled the mug up to her mouth.

His father peered over in her direction raising his brow. She shot back a warning glare, before smiling awkwardly, and taking another sip of her toxic brew.

He found it amusing that his parents did not think he knew that his mother's coffee was laced with a spirit of some sort. He also knew that was not her first shot that morning. He smirked to himself as he dived into his breakfast. He had places to be today, and he was excited to finally visit the record company that would be producing his first single.

'Morning!' Jed rushed into the kitchen stuffing a spare piece of toast into his mouth.

'Jed! It's almost 10am!' his father scolded.

'I know, I know, I'm late. I accidentally knocked my alarm off!'

'It pays to keep good time, son.'

'See you all later!' Jed called, ignoring his father's advice, 'Oh, Dan, good luck today!'

Dan beamed and gave his brother a thumbs up as he shovelled most of his beans into his mouth.

A burning sensation forced its way up from his stomach, his mouth overflowing with saliva. Dan tried to swallow it back, but like trying to empty a sinking boat, it was no good. The taste of vomit tickled the back of his throat before emerging from the depths to partially choke him. He threw himself forward over the side of the bed. His stomach bruised; intense contractions had left him feeling weak. He felt cold but was sweating, he lurched forward again spraying the floor with chunky partially digested food. His face was flushed, he breathed in deep to regain some control. He caught a glimpse of his reflection in the mirrored door of his wardrobe. *What a sight*. He hung his head over the mess, slime dangling from his chin.

Forcing himself, Dan finally managed to sit upright. His stomach still churning. He stayed there staring at himself in the mirror, he noticed his face was not as full as it once was, his eyes were blood shot and slightly sunken. He looked frail and old beyond his years. With the room spinning around him, he was not quite ready to pull himself up onto his feet, but there was a dim glow of determination urging him forward.

He stared closer into his sunken, blood shot eyes. They were still a vibrant blue, even though they no longer had that topaz sparkle which could charm anyone who was captured by them.

An idea rippled over him to get outside for some fresh air, maybe go for a walk or get a greasy bacon roll from that new bakery in town he had heard good things about it. Maybe it would curb his hangover? That was soon dismissed by his ting demons, they challenged him to get a shower, put on some clothes and walk out the front door. *Just imagine the looks* he heard them tease. They were right, he was still recognised by those who still praised him. How disappointed they would be to see him like this? They would whisper between one another, making snide comments just loud enough for him to hear. Dan stared into the mirror again, taunted by the reflection staring back at him.

Dan often walked into town, or to the local shop just minutes from his home. Not fazed by the fact that he would be recognised by someone, and then someone else, the domino effect often followed. He would hear giggles behind him, *look who it is … is it really him?* But when they finally conjured up enough courage to speak to him, it was his eyes that would render them speechless, like they had cast an instant silent spell. Their faces would flush into a ruby glow, before asking him awkwardly for a photo.

He missed the spontaneous interaction with his fans. It was a little unsettling at times when they prowled behind him, but in a way, it was also quite flattering that they went out of their way to be noticed by him.

The thought made him smile, he felt a faint tingle moving up through him, a welcoming warmth surging upwards and filling his chest, but suddenly it turned, it became heavier, forcing its way through. A wave of nausea struck him down, his stomach tightened, violently contracting, stomach acid bubbled promising another aggressive eruption, and it wasn't backing down, he could feel the rancid vomit clawing its way back up through his throat. *Oh no, not again.*

His head hit the pillow with a heavy thud. As he closed his eyes, he was greeted by a familiar face that brought more pain than the regurgitated whiskey. It was a pain he carried with him every day, but it was only triggered when he was reminded of *her*.

03 – Mother Knows Best

He jumped up to the deep thumps echoing down the hallway. He lifted his head in confusion, opening one eye. Maybe he dreamt it? A few minutes later he heard it again, only more prominent, with each bang getting louder. He really didn't have the energy to get up. He flopped back into his pillow, 'maybe if I ignore it… it will stop,' he convinced himself. He lay there on his side, still and silent. Listening. He heard the creak of the letterbox…

'Hello?' said the voice, which bounced down the walls.

He groaned and rolled over onto his front, grabbing a pillow opposite him, he dumped it onto his already pounding head. *Ow. Have they gone yet?* He waited, smothered under his pillow.

'I know you're in there.' The voice revealed.

Damn it. He kicked the covers down toward the end of the bed with his feet and slowly sat up and caressed his pulsing head.

'Hello?' The voice repeated.

Urgh. Why won't they go away? He steadily lifted himself to his feet, feeling a little lightheaded and wobbly he managed to stumble down the hallway to the front door.

'Who is it?' Dan raised his voice, peering through the spy hole, silently fighting a debate with himself whether to remove the latch. He rested his head hard against the door. *I could really do without this today. Why is she even here?* He muttered to himself.

Dan had not even got the door open an inch and she barged her way through, he stumbled, the sudden movement made his pounding head spin, reviving the burning in his throat, it forced him to breath in deep desperate not to let it overtake him.

'Jesus … please Mother, do come in,' he said, holding his head to help stop the walls spinning around him.

'Wow, you look … Erm ...' she thought carefully about the words that followed, '… good night?' she asked. 'Oh my god! What *is* that smell?' She leaned a little closer to him and sniffed, then turned in the direction of his bedroom. She walked closer to the door, the smell grew stronger, a sour stale stench of alcohol. She covered her nose and mouth with both hands, and quickly pulled the collar of her jacket over her face.

She turned round to face him. He was just standing there staring blankly at the ground, his body swaying ever so slightly. She held back the impulse to scold him, instead she sighed and rubbed her forehead. She walked back towards him and placed her handbag just by the front door, 'Okay! ... Kitchen, please. You need coffee, and a lot of it by the looks of you, and we need to get what's left of your stomach lined!' She motioned her hands, shooing him forward. 'Come, on,' she ordered, the contents of the Tesco's bag for life rustled together as she sped down the hallway ahead of him.

Dan followed her to the kitchen slowly. Stopping to steady himself every so often. He really didn't want any food; he knew that his stomach would immediately refuse the offering and return it sharpish. He felt compelled to do as he was asked, he was never any good at refusing his mother's demands. She had been incredibly involved early in his career, taking her role as manager very seriously. She had control of what he would wear, where he performed and, which functions he'd attend. He had slightly resented the fact that he had little control over it, but if he had listened, maybe things wouldn't have turned out the way they did. He stood in the doorway and leaned his body against the frame, watching his mother as she shuffled about in the kitchen, his head enjoying the brief cold of the wooden frame.

She paused, noticing the empty bottles dumped by the sink, they glared at her, still holding the scent of their old contents, shaking her head to herself she started to empty her Tesco bag, half full of groceries. She knew he would not have had anything remotely edible for her to cook for him, so she came prepared. She also knew he didn't want her here, but that was just tough luck, he needed her. She could feel his eyes burning a hole into her back, but she did not care. She was not about to let him fall down the same bumpy road as she did. She searched the cupboard for the frying pan and put it on the stove ready for the bacon and eggs she had just unpacked. The empty bottles beckoned the demons of her past, *do you remember* …

Ruth had forced her glass towards the end of the bench, it was slowing her down. She didn't even hear it fall. Glass fragments scattered across the floor, she looked at the mess, her eyes weighing down her face. Lines of mascara smeared across her cheeks; her freshly lined lips were now a blurred stain. She crouched by the foot of the breakfast bar, cradling her vodka bottle and wept...

She had returned home earlier after a meeting at the record label, they expressed their ongoing concerns, and it was likely that they would be releasing Dan from his contract. This was all she needed. It did not look like her husband had finished work yet. Over the last few months, he had been working late, having more business meetings.

She wasn't going to let that bother her, just one shot more and she would laugh about it, no harm done. Today though, she needed him, she needed to get a lot off her chest, hopeful that he would offer a resolution, how do they deal with Dan now?

I'll probably get the blame, she told herself as she dumped her bag on to the nearest chair and hurried over to the coffee machine. She reached up into one of the higher cabinets and pulled out the first bottle she touched and poured a fair amount into the bottom of her mug. She tapped her manicured nails against the marble worktop as she waited for the coffee to come to a boil and noticed a piece of paper. *Typical, I bet that's him telling me another out-of-town meeting has come up!* She opened the note with a huff.

Ruth,

There was never going to be an easy way to say this. I just can't do this anymore.

I'm sorry.

I want a divorce.

J x

Reading those last four words, left her winded, like someone had just come at her with a knife. The kiss at the end was the final twist in her gut. She struggled to breathe, her heart thumped hard against her chest, her legs weakened and gave way beneath her, she fell onto her side, her hands slapping the cold tiled floor on contact. She lay there silent for a moment and let out a piercing scream that echoed throughout the house. She needed to numb this pain the only way she knew how. She pulled herself back up in front on of the coffee machine and reached up to the higher cabinets and pulled out a bottle of vodka...

'Mum?' Jed said gently as he approached her.

Ruth quickly wiped her tears and disguised her blotchy face with a smile, 'careful, the glass, Love!' She sobbed as Jed attempted to get to her.

Jed stopped abruptly, scanning the floor, and moved carefully round the shards on tipped toe, he settled on the floor next to his mother and draped his arms over her.

She rested her head on his shoulders, 'don't you worry, I'm fine, I'll be okay.'

Shaking off her haunting demons, she blinked back into the reality with a jump. Smoke had started to fill the room, the oil spitting furiously at her, demanding attention. She turned the flame down quickly and waved her hand through the smoke and reached over the sink to crack open the window. She shuffled the pan and checked the eggs, which had started to brown round the edge. *Damn it, I always burn the eggs!*

'Come on, sit down,' she called gleefully and gestured him towards the dining table, 'it's nearly ready'.

Ruth sat for a short while and watched him guide the beans around his plate with a fork. She left him to silently dissect his breakfast so she could search under the sink for cleaning products.

04 – That's What Mothers Do

Ruth lingered by the bedroom door clutching a bucket she had filled with a little hot water, and a bottle of disinfectant. She had several cloths stuffed under her arm and had readily armed herself with a pair of rubber gloves, though she wished she had some sort of mask or a peg for her nose at least. She took in a deep breath and slowly creaked open the door. The room was dark, musky, and stale. She set the bucket down by the door and walked over towards the windows. This room needed an injection of daylight, it must have been some time since these curtains had been opened. As soon as she pulled them back, a snow like mist twinkled around her. She pushed open each of the windows to let in some fresh air.

Her eyes gave the room a once over. There was a large pile of clothes in the far corner, dumped in a messy heap. Empty bottles were abandoned by the side of the bed. Cigarette ash dusted the surface of the side table. The sight was nearly enough to distract her from the smell.

She threw a large cloth into the bucket and swirled it round in the water and rang it out, placing it close by. She held her breath as she started to scoop up the lumps that had now sunk into the carpet, holding her breath as she did so. She paused to breath into her shoulder, trying desperately not to take in too deep a breath. She had thought the days of cleaning up after her children were long gone, especially this sort of mess, yet here she was on all fours scooping up chunks of God knows what with her hands, very thankful for the rubber gloves.

She did the best she could, she covered the area with a thin layer of disinfectant and worked it into the carpet. The vapours aggravated her eyes, but at least that awful smell had been disguised somewhat. After she scrubbed the carpet to an inch of its life she placed the used cloths into the bucket, and popped it outside the bedroom door, she couldn't take that into the kitchen while he was eating. She turned her attention to the dusty side table and the heap of clothes, *well as I am already here, cleaning up sick from the floor, I might as well,* she thought and made her way towards the kitchen sink and removed her gloves.

'How are you getting on?' she asked him.

'I really can't eat this.'

'Well at least try the orange juice, get some vitamin C in you,' she said as she rummaged through the cupboard for polish and a duster.

'I can't,' he mumbled.

Ruth ignored his groans as she made her way back to his bedroom and dived into her next challenge.

She didn't notice him standing in the doorway as she sorted through the pile, a lot of the clothes she decided needed to be rewashed, some needed ironing, and the rest needed the bin.

'You don't need to do that you know,' he said eventually, 'I would have done it.'

She didn't believe him, especially as these clothes looked like they had been laying here a lot longer than a week.

'It's okay.' she replied. 'It's like old times,' she joked.

He looked back at her with a slightly confused expression. He couldn't recall her ever being this positive cleaning his room when he lived at home. He remembered her always complaining about the state he left things in, *does this live here? No? Pick this up! Put that back, now!*

'This pile here needs washing,' she patted the top of the pile beside her. 'I'll put a load on for you now'.

Dan smiled awkwardly and thanked her, quietly thinking to himself how grateful he was.

He caught a glimpse of himself in the mirror as his mother began bundling the pile for the wash in her arms. His hair was now a dull greasy clump stuck to the top of his head and resembled the texture of one of those cheese string snacks children take in their packed lunches; he probably didn't smell far from one either.

He glanced to the reflection of the bed and saw the empty bottles now placed upright on his bedside table. He stood quietly counting them in his head, feeling an urge to explain that he hadn't drank them all in one night, but he didn't feel that justified as an excuse, given what he was letting her put herself through. His rapidly beating heart thumped aggressively, giving him a sharp inward jab. He rubbed his chest. His mother was here clearing up his life, while she was still fighting for her own. The bottles taunting her while she worked around them. *How does she do it? Where has her sudden strength come from?*

'Why don't you jump in the shower while I'm here? Freshen up a bit?' She suggested.

The sudden outburst of her voice startled him. The corners of his mouth turned up slightly.

'A shower might be nice,' he agreed and turned slowly towards the door.

'I'm sorry.' he said turning back to her.

Ruth smiled back gently, 'It's not your fault love,' she assured him and started walking down the hall balancing the messy bundle of clothes in her arms. 'If anything, it's *mine*,' she whispered, forcing back the sting in her eyes.

Dan emerged from the bathroom surrounded by a huge curtain of steam, which escaped out the door before him. He felt clean and refreshed, it felt good, even the pounding in his head had subsided. The pain in his stomach was now nothing but dull ache that twinged sharply every now and then just as a subtle reminder that it was still in recovery. He ruffled a towel through his hair, stopping as he noticed the bed was made, with fresh sheets, and a pair of jeans, a T-shirt, underwear, and socks were placed in a line at the end of the bed.

Jesus. How long was I in there for? Dan scanned his room slowly. Nothing was out of place, the sides were dusted and cleared, the floor had been decluttered, although a rather large area was now noticeably damp, and it looked like it had been vacuumed, but he didn't recall hearing the vacuum cleaner. The room had a faint floral scent to it now and was filled with a cool breeze rushing in from opened windows. He smiled, shaking his head in disbelief, he had almost questioned if he had walked into the same room, Mother is on a mission! A flicker of gratitude escaped the corner of his mouth.

Dan heard the motion of the washing machine slowly slushing its contents in a half-hearted spin as he walked towards the kitchen and loitered in the doorway. He saw his mother sat at the dining table staring into her mug, of what he hoped, was just coffee, or maybe she drank tea now? He wasn't sure, he hadn't seen that much of her. He had walked into this image of her many times as a child. She still caressed the mug the same way, she rested the mug on her lips. Ruth had been in recovery now for a little over 8 years and it made her see life in a whole new light. Alcohol free. Until she came here. Today she has faced nothing but torment from the same empty bottles she had fought so hard against. The guilt knocked him again, a little harder this time. He rubbed his chest, *Shit. I hope I've not just pushed her off the wagon!* He shook his head dismissively.

Ruth's phone started skipping in circles on the table dancing round to its silent disco, it finally grabbed her attention as it made its way over to the edge. Jumping to catch it before it fell, her arm brushed against her mug, knocking it on its side, a mocha river rushed out, spreading across the table. She scurried over to the sink, grabbed a spare cloth and dashed back over.

'Good lord, you frightened me! How long have you been standing there?' Ruth shrieked as she spotted him in the doorway, stopping in her tracks as if she had just slammed on an emergency brake. She placed her hand over her chest to calm her pounding heart and took in a deep breath.

'Not that long, just got dressed … what was in that?' Dan nodded his head towards the turned over mug. He raised his eyebrow at her, as he often did when he was preparing to fire back a dose of sarcasm.

'Just coffee, love. I needed a little surge of energy after all that scrubbing.' Ruth smiled awkwardly and glanced over at the large puddle now waterfalling onto the floor. 'Ooh, don't worry, I'll see to that now! Sorry, love!'

Dan exhaled relief. He had no reason to question her, after all she had done for him today, and he couldn't be a hypocrite and accuse her of adding a little extra heat to her rewarding brew… could he? As he watched her soak up the mess, he put the thought to the back of his mind. He was sure he left not even a drop in any of those bottles, even if she were lured into temptation. He felt quite smug with himself.

Ruth's phone illuminated again, buzzing frantically, she stretched over the table for one final sweep, capturing any spots she might have missed and reached for her phone. Ruth awkwardly offered Dan an, "sorry-I-have-to-take-this" smile, before answering the call.

'Hello, Love. Are you okay? … That's good …yes … um… no… not yet … no … yes, I'm just with your brother, no, just me … its fine, I'll call you later, okay? … pretty bad …no, I'm okay…' Her eyes glanced to Dan again before continuing her conversation, 'honestly, I'm fine, everything is fine … I will call you later okay, Love?... I'll be sure to tell him, maybe not quite how you said it but... okay, yes, okay ... bye Love.' Ruth exhaled dramatically and smiled at him, 'your brother sends his love.'

Dan raised his eyebrows. *Yeah. Sure, he does.* 'What was he calling for?' He asked, rather abruptly.

'Oh ... he was ... just checking in,' she shrugged like it was nothing, 'he often does.'

He couldn't help but wonder if that was a subtle dig at him. He never called her. He never really had anything to talk about or want to talk about for that. His evening companion often gave him a nasty tongue, so it was probably in his mother's best interests that he didn't contact her for needless chatter. He would never give a second thought to how he hurt people with his sharp words, nor would he show a blink of remorse in the moment. The following day he would never remember what he had said and would carry on as normal. Oblivious to any carnage he caused. It never happened. In his mind, people left his life on their own accord. *He* had done nothing wrong. If you can't remember, it didn't happen, right?

'Come on, put on your shoes.' She spoke with an excited tone as if she were addressing a toddler, 'we need to fill these cupboards with something edible... probably best I drive though.' She smiled and walked off to collect her bag.

He rolled his eyes at her, *what is she so upbeat about?* He hadn't left the house in weeks; people would see him. They would talk and whisper behind him, and not in a cute fit of giggles. They would be judging him, criticising him. He was not sure if he was ready to face the outside world. His hands became sweaty, and his heart was beating like he had just completed a marathon. He placed his arm on the counter next to him and rested his head down.

'Everything okay?' His mother had reappeared with her bag and another unsettling smile. *Why was she so happy? I don't think I have seen her smile so much in one day!* The way he felt after his shower had most definitely rubbed off, or maybe the pulsing hangover was beginning to mess with his head. Dan followed her reluctantly to the driveway and hopped into the passenger side of her red Nissan Qashqai. The interior was furnished with leather seats and was a cold shock to sit on. He rubbed his arms frantically to try and feel some warmth.

'Maybe, you should have grabbed a jumper!' Ruth laughed, 'the seats are heated, here.' She flicked a button in front of the gear stick, he felt a faint warm sensation around him. 'Let me know when you are warm enough, and I'll turn it off, it can get a bit too toasty sometimes.'

Ruth still had that weird smile painted on her face

as she turned the ignition. *What is up with her?* Dan wondered to himself.

There was something very tranquil about a moving a car, the motion was soothing and the warmth from the seat made it far too easy to imagine you were tucked up in bed. Dan rested his head against the cold window and took in the view, hypnotised by trees and buildings … and trees and buildings … and trees …

05 – Take Me Home

'I think I dozed off there,' he yawned, stretching his arms out, pushing against the roof of the car. He glanced over to the digital clock in the head unit. He was confused. They were still driving. Dan was sure the nearest supermarket was no more than 10 or 15 minutes away from his home. It looked like they had been driving for more than half an hour, at least. Dan sat forward and looked at his mother. 'Erm … Tell me just how far is this supermarket you're taking me to?' Dan questioned.

Ruth shifted in her seat and side eyed him in silence, then returned her attention to the road.

Dan waited anxiously for a reply. 'Well?' He prompted.

Silence.

His hands started shaking as he glared at his mother, the frown lines on his forehead becoming more prominent. 'MUM!' He erupted, making her jerk the steering wheel.

Her heart pounded as she straightened up, 'for goodness' sake!' She gasped at him 'look this is for your own good, I have your best interests at heart, honestly, I do. This is what you need! Trust me, I know'.

What the bloody hell was she talking about? He looked at her puzzled, anger bubbled from his gut, turning his face a fierce red. He thought for a moment he might be sick again. 'WHERE ARE WE GOING?' He demanded; his shaking hands slowly forming a tight fist. He saw the weird smile she had painted on her face twitch slightly; he could see water fill her eyes and trickle slowly down her cheek.

She worked on her breathing, before answering him, and cleared her throat. 'We're all worried about you. You don't leave the house; you drink more than you eat, and that's if you even eat at all! You are not looking after yourself. I know the signs. You need help.'

Help? She had already come round uninvited, cooking and cleaning… was that not helping? What is she getting at? 'Who's *we*?' Dan tutted and raised his brow.

'Well, your brother and I were-'

'My Brother?!' He interrupted with a chuckle, 'Oh I cannot believe this. What the hell does he know about my life? I don't even remember the last time I had a conversation with him, I am the shit stain of the family after all. What does he have to do with all this?' He looked at his mother expecting her to respond with something, but she stayed quiet, 'I bet this was his idea, wasn't it? Kidnap me from my home. You come in and play the concerned mother role, and take me to an unknown location? Tie me up and torture me because you don't approve of my lifestyle? I must say Mother, your acting skills have improved, bravo. You had me fooled back there for a while. You might as well bump me off now and get it over with.'

'Don't be ridiculous, your brother loves you!'

'HA! Yes of course he does!' He rolled his eyes.

'He does. I love you … We all do. We want what is best for you. We want to help you get better.'

'Get better? There's nothing bloody wrong with me!'

'It's nothing to be ashamed of, it's a disease. I got through it, and you will too.' she strained a smile.

Dan screwed his face at her, 'I'm nothing like you, Mother!' He snarled. 'I don't add any s*pecial* ingredients to my coffee. I don't need to. I don't carry a fucking, no-bar-in-the-area-emergency-flask around with me, and I certainly don't start my day with a shot of tequila and a forced smile. I'm fine, so what if I have a drink of an evening, who doesn't!' He leaned towards her, 'take me home,' he ordered in a low heavy growl.

Ruth ignored him, 'look, I understand denial more than anyone, it took your dad leaving to make me to see I had a problem, but it gave me the kick up the arse to get the help I needed. If I had carried on …'

'And how is dad?' he smirked.

Dan's dad, James Hayes, had started a new relationship not long after he left Ruth. He was likely having an affair, although he swore blindly that he was honourable and faithful throughout his marriage. Dan knew that even now, after all these years, it hurt his mother to be reminded that the man she married, the father of her children, went off to have a life with someone else.

Ruth thought that breaking herself free from the reliance of alcohol would be all she needed to do to get him back, but he had no interest, he said to her, 'give you two weeks, you will be back on the vodka!' Ruth was desperate to prove him wrong, prove them all wrong.

Ruth couldn't bring herself to say anything. She kept her watery eyes on the road. She knew he wasn't going to be happy about this road trip and she had prepared herself for the back lash of nasty comments. At least … she assured herself she had.

'Right, Mother, come on. I have had enough of this shit now. You were to blame for your husband leaving you. *You* know it. *We* know it, the *world* knows it. We're sorry, you know, but shit happens, we move on. But what you *really* need to do right now, is take me home, okay, just take me *home*.'

'How dare you,' she wheezed, wiping her face with one hand as more tears fell, 'you think you were blameless!' She half laughed, 'it was you and your fucking antics that pushed me too far! I struggled more and more to keep you from ruining what you had worked so hard for. Thinking you were above everyone, doing whatever the fuck you wanted, hurting people. You weren't aware of how many hours of meetings I had dealt with begging that label not to kick you out on your arse. You thought you were untouchable. If it weren't for me, you wouldn't have had any sort of career at all. Drinking was the only escape I had from all the stress I took on with that job, it took the edge off everything. You have no idea of the sacrifice I made for you.'

'If it wasn't for *you*, I wouldn't have a career? Is that what you just said? It's because of *you* I *don't* have a career!' Dan glared at her, 'you made yourself my manager, that was your job. You chose to do that, I didn't ask you to take over, did I? Anyway, you were paid weren't you, and we all know what you spent the money on… and mine for that, don't think I don't know that you dipped in and out of *my* money whenever you fancied – why spend your own when you have access to the millions your son has in the bank!'

'I didn't take a thing!' Ruth snapped, 'That's your dad, filling your head with shit before he left, but you know what you can bloody believe what you like.'

Dan grinned at her and raised his brow, 'An escape, was it, drinking? I'd like to escape from this fucking car, what do you say we go find a pub and get shit faced, some proper Mother, Son bonding!' He suggested loudly rubbing his hands together, 'come on, old girl, what do you say? I'll even buy the first round, Vodka, is it?'

She wiped her face again and quickly moved it back to change gear and indicated her intention to go right at the roundabout.

'No? ... well then, here's another thought ... TAKE ME HOME!'

Ruth ignored him again, this conversation was getting bitter and hurtful, and a little too much to handle now. She stayed silent and concentrated on the oncoming traffic to her right, waited for a clear opening and accelerated.

Anger possessed him, 'I said - TAKE ME HOME!' he lunged forward and forced the steering wheel from her hands, his rage blinding him from his surroundings.

His mother squealed through tears, 'NO! ... STOP! ... WHAT THE FUCK ARE YOU DOING?'

Ruth tried to take Dan's hands from the wheel. The car hit the curb of the roundabout with a clunk. The car sprung upwards, flipping it heavily onto its side. Dan was thrown back into his seat, slamming into the passenger door panel. His head crashed against the glass sending a sharp jolt of pain straight to his eyes. His vision became blurred, his ears were ringing, but he managed to make out an echoing blast of a lorry horn before he was thrust back on the crunch of impact. Ruth's car was pushed along on its side while the desperate lorry driver slammed his brakes to a screeching halt.

The last thing Dan heard as the lorry carried them was his mother's scream. There was nothing now but silence, the buzzing in his ears had nearly deafened him, he could make out blurred shapes moving towards the car. He heard muffled voices but couldn't make out any words, and then white noise filled his head. He peered over to his mother and tried hard to speak, but no words came out, his breathing becoming more of a struggle. Ruth was still, lifeless, her blurred face covered in a red blotch. Pain shot through him, a sting formed in his eyes, hot tears rushed down his face. He urged her to be okay, he *needed* her to be okay. *What have I done?* His eyes grew heavier, the shadows surrounded him, slowly blending into darkness.

06 – The After Effect

'Where are you going now? I thought we were going to talk?' Kara's eyes gave a warning glisten, her cheeks reddened, and her bottom lip started to tremble. She placed her hand on her chest to soothe the growing lump of anxiety that was threatening to close off her airways. 'I don't understand!' She sobbed, placing her hand over her belly.

Dan gave her nothing but an empty stare and a cold shrug of the shoulders, he turned away from her and walked out the door, forcing her to watch him disappear down the street. She called after him several times, begging him for him to come back. One of the neighbours stuck their head out of their front door to show their disapproving scowl and huffed as they slammed their door closed. Dan sniggered at them, *nosey bastards*.

He slipped around a corner, so he was out of Kara's sight and took out his phone from his back jean pocket, 'o'right, mate? Yes, I escaped,' Dan chuckled, 'see you in 10?'

'Hey, what are you doing down there?' Ruth smiled as she poked her head under the duvet fort which Dan had draped over two chairs.

'Playing,' Dan replied.

'Ah, but what are you playing?' she asked curiously.

Dan giggled at her as he presented two toy cars, 'they're racing!' He zoomed towards her making "vroom vroom" noises. 'Oh, no! This one is losing control!' He yelled, 'It's gonna craaaaashhh!' He made a high-pitched screeching sound as he toppled over onto his side, 'did you see that Mummy?' Dan looked up for her, 'Mummy? … Where are you?' He stuck his head out of the entrance to his fort. His vision blurred as he crawled out. He squinted. He could make out a figure sat in a chair. He squeezed his eyes a bit tighter and creeped closer, he could see smears of red across their face. He stiffened, careful not to startle them. He rubbed his eyes like he was trying to ease an irritating itch and sighed as his vision cleared.

Dan slowly returned his attention to the mysterious figure sat on the chair in his bedroom. An ice-cold wave of fear washed over him, he took a deep breath and looked towards the chair. It was a woman, her faced was puffy, bruised and reddened by the blood dripping from a large wound on her forehead. Her eyes began to flicker, and she said his name in a grim manner, 'look what you have done to me!' she breathed.

He cried out, 'Mummy!' Tears rapidly falling down his face, forcing him to drop to his knees. He muttered he was sorry over and over to himself and he curled up tightly into a ball and fell into darkness.

'Come on, mate, this one is yours!' Dan looked up to his friend swaying in front of him, then glanced around the room of people he didn't recognise. Most were women who wanted to be noticed, with their midriff bare and wide smiles, eyes scanning the room for a target.

His heart felt like it was knocking against his rib cage, his mouth felt numb and sweat bubbled on his forehead.

'Mate!' his friend tugged hard on his arm and his body jerked into the direction he was being dragged in. He followed his friend to a table on the far side of a large and very bright white and grey kitchen. He was placed in front of a fluffy, snow-white line and handed a rolled up £10 note.

'Get on it, mate!' his friend gave him an

encouraging pat on the back before swaying off, hollering towards two girls downing pints of beer.

Dan casually accepted the burning powder and held his nose to subside the sting. He sniffed again and wiped his nose on the back of his hand, then turned his attention to the "oohs" that were growing louder through the crowd.

'He's not here love, go home,' Dan heard as he stumbled through the doorway.

'What are you doing here woman?' Dan slurred at her.

Kara stared at his dripping face and bulging eyes 'what have you taken now?' she asked, grabbing his face to get a closer look at his dilated pupils, 'please just come home.'

'I...'

Dan stopped to steady his balance.

'I am not… going … ANYWHERE.' Dan pointed an unsteady finger at her as he sniffed and smiled coyly, 'with YOU!' He roared triumphantly at her, and the crowd cheered around him.

'Please Dan, this isn't you.'

'Then who am I then?' he asked waving his arms at her.

She shrugged her shoulders, 'you're not this person. These people aren't your friends.'

'Just fuck off, will ya!' he slurred, shoving her away from him. They both stumbled backwards.

'Yeah, you tell her, mate!' Dan heard someone applaud.

Kara regained her balance quickly with the aid of a chair close by. Dan took a tumble, tripping over the back of his trainer, he laughed it off as two girls tugged on his arms and helped him to his feet. Kara tried to push passed the lump in her throat, but she struggled to hold onto her pride and disappeared quickly with her sobs echoing behind her.

'Bye, darling! Thanks for coming!' someone laughed.

He flinched awake as he felt a throbbing pressure on the side of his head, pain pulsated through his shoulder and down the left side of his body. He was surrounded by a faint beeping, he strained to lift his eyelids, only managing to open them slightly. The lights stung, forcing them closed again. *Bloody hell must have drunk a hell of a lot last night.* The bed didn't feel like his own, it was smaller, his elbows poked out over each side.

Beep … beep … beep … beep

Ugh, what was that annoying sound? He managed to force his eyes open halfway … this was not his bedroom; this room was bright white – clean and smelt of disinfectant strong enough to taste.

Beep … beep … beep … beep

Dan lifted his hand to his head to soothe his confusion, 'Ow! Shit! What the hell?!'

'Ah, you are awake, good.' Came a voice from the other side of the room.

He gaped at a man in a long white overcoat standing at the foot of his bed. 'Where am I? … Who are you?' Dan muttered. *Bastards have knocked me out and put me in a dodgy clinic haven't they.*

'You're in hospital.' He replied. 'My name is Dr Creed, 'I've been monitoring you since you arrived yesterday,' Dr Creed explained.

'Yesterday?' Dan repeated.

'You should know the police have been, they have requested to speak with you.'

'The Police?!' Dan gasped. 'Why?!' He stared at the doctor intently, waiting for his response.

'What do you remember?' Dr Creed asked curiously.

Dan took a minute, trying to piece together a memory. 'I …. I was …. I was with my mum …. We were in the car … she … wait is my mum here? Did she bring me here?' he stared wide eyed.

Dr Creed stood professionally, 'you and your mother were involved in a car accident.' Dr Creed explained.

He shut his eyes tight. 'We … Accident?' He screwed his face in disbelief *'no'* he whispered to himself. 'Where is she? … Is she okay?' his chest now pained with guilt.

'We are doing everything we can for her.' Dr Creed assured, 'now, I just need to run a few routine checks on you, and I'll leave you to rest.'

Dr Creed took Dan's arm, which was limp, lifeless, and numb. He only just felt his arm being squeezed as Dr

Creed took his blood pressure. He stared at the wall opposite, he felt the pain throbbing in his head, he could hear it pulsing. Sound faded. The Doctor mentioned something to him before he left the room, but all he heard was a deep muffle.

'Please, Sir!' A muffled voice pleaded as heavy footsteps stormed towards the door, 'He needs to rest!'

'Like shit he needs to rest.' Came the reply.

The door to his room swung open so fast it rebounded from the stoppers with a bang so loud anyone would have mistaken it for a gunshot. Dan jumped. His brother, Jed was charging towards him with a scolding red face and with disgust in his eyes. His breathing was deep and sharp, almost like he was growling. He wiped his hand over his face.

'What the hell is wrong with you?!' Jed spat, 'She's in there …' His voice trailed off. He growled as he fought the cocktail of emotion brewing in his gut.

Dan sat paralysed, staring at his brother as Jed hurled each word of revulsion towards him, anything he could to make just that little bit worse about himself. He took each blow with no retaliation as his brother swung a few more rounds.

'It should be you fighting for your life!' Jed roared.

Dan's mind wandered, trying to remember how they crashed. *Was it really my fault?*

'… And all you got was a few fucking broken ribs and a dislocated shoulder …' Jed was still spiralling off curse words at him as a woman entered the room.

'Honey, calm down this won't help anyone.'

Her voice was familiarly comforting, kind and reassuring. The heaviness in the room lifted the moment she spoke. It stopped his brother dead in his vile character assassination. The room was quiet again.

'Hi, Dan,' she said in her angelic tone.

Dan looked up. It was *her*. She was back. *She came back … I was so cruel to her.* His heart pounded; butterflies swirled. He smiled … *Kara … no … wait a minute…* his face dropped, 'did you just call him honey?' he said, keeping his eyes on her. Her eyes danced round the room but refused to meet his.

'I'm sorry sir, I'm going to have to ask you to leave, you are disturbing some of our patients in the other rooms.' came a voice from the nurse standing in the doorway.

'Pfft,' Jed turned towards the nurse. 'Fed up with the bloody sight of him anyway.'

Jed glanced back at Dan sat in the hospital bed. He hadn't taken his eyes off Kara.

'This isn't over'. Jed warned, 'stay the fuck away from Mum...' He wrapped his arm firmly around Kara's shoulders, '... and her too for that, you fucking psycho'. Jed led Kara out of the room, she kept her head down, still refusing eye contact and allowed his so-called brother to guide her out the door.

'*Prick.*' Dan muttered under his breath.

'Are you okay, Mr Hayes?' the nurse asked, still stood in the doorway.

'Yeah … Thanks.' Dan said, trying to sound convincing.

The nurse offered a sympathetic smile, 'if you need anything, just ring the bell and someone will see to you.' She gestured her head towards the buzzer by the side of his bed.

'Will, do.' Dan nodded. 'Oh actually, is there any chance I could get a TV … it's a bit quiet in here now.'

'There should be one in here.' The nurse answered. She walked towards the bed, pulling a small rectangular screen on a long-armed wall mount. 'I am afraid they aren't the biggest of TVs,' she laughed. She showed him how to flick between channels before she left, not that there was much choice. Dan just chose to watch the channel with the clearest picture, he wasn't too bothered about what was on. He just wanted to fill the silence.

'... Lastly, the two people who were involved in a severe car accident yesterday, have now been identified as Daniel Hayes and his mother and former manager, Ruth Hayes. They have both been admitted to hospital where they are being treated for their injuries. We wish them both a full and speedy recovery.'

Oh shit. He let his head fall into his hands. *Ow.*

He reached over to the buzzer that summoned a nurse, although it was some time after he pressed it that anyone came tohis aid.

'Mr Hayes is everything okay?' The nurse asked.

'Can I have some pain killers?' He asked holding his head.

The nurse walked over to the foot of his bed and checked his notes. 'Yep, looks like you are due for some. I'll bring them through.' She smiled.

'Thank you ... erm ... another thing, could I see my mum? Or could someone tell me how she is?'

The nurse nodded, 'I'm sure that can be arranged, I'll just get you your medication, Mr Hayes and I will request for someone to come over to talk to you.'

She returned with several pills in a small white pot that resembled a shot glass and handed it to him. He didn't bother asking what they were, he knocked them back with the fresh water the nurse had offered and fell back onto his pillow and hoped that they kicked in quickly.

'Dr Creed will be along to speak with you soon. He is just with another patient now, but he will be along shortly.' the nurse told him as she took back his empty pill cup.

Dr Creed walked into the room about an hour later, 'Mr Hayes, I understand that you have been asking about your mother?'

Dan nodded at him eagerly and waited.

'Well, I will be honest it was touch and go when she arrived, but she is stable now, and all is looking good, I'll spare you the medical blurb given what you've been through, but she's doing well, and she has been asking after you too. She wanted to know that you were safe and wants to see you as soon as possible, but may I suggest we maybe leave that for tomorrow. You both need rest.'

'Thank you, Doctor,' Dan smiled. Dr Creed bowed his head, dismissing himself.

That night Dan struggled to settle, pain surged up

and down his body whenever he moved, the slightest twitch would send another bolt through him. His head pounded and felt like it had doubled in size. They wouldn't give him anything else for the pain, or anything to help him sleep, he had already had his rations for the day. Dan pressed the button on the side of the bed to raise the pillow end slightly, *bit better*, he thought. He felt a little less pressure down his side which helped ease the pain somewhat. He stared at the far wall for a while as a focus point as he lay back into a state of diminished tranquillity.

07 – Girl At The Bar

Dan first met Kara at a nightclub, he was in his early 20's, not long before he was dropped from his record label, according to the headlines, which he swore blind was inaccurate. He would call out journalists online, mainly on twitter, and anyone else who would dare to have an opinion he didn't approve of. Although Dan no longer had a single in the charts, he still had a large following. Living behind old pictures, sharing stories reminding people who he was. It was not unusual for him to be stopped out in public. Dan would use the opportunity to brag about new projects he was working on that didn't exist, still trying to keep himself relevant. His followers would gaze at him in awe. He would often go out with old members of his band, it gave the perfect impression that he was working on new music, without having to say anything.

Music vibrated through his body as he moved through a wave of stretched arms swaying to the rhythm. 'WHAT ARE WE DRINKING BOYS?!' Dan shouted over his shoulder. 'TOBY! YOUR ROUND MATE!'

'YOU DON'T HAVE TO KEEP A RECORD!' Toby laughed as he barked everyone's request at the bar tender. Dan glanced round the room, while he waited for his drink, his eyes were drawn to a girl perched up on a stool at the end of the bar. She was sat on her own, sipping a drink through a straw and nodding her head along with the music with her eyes closed.

'SEE ANY TARGETS?' Toby shouted in Dan's ear as he handed him a dripping cold bottle, 'WE'RE GOING TO THROW YOU IN THAT GROUP OF GIRLS OVER THERE!' He pointed a little too obviously, 'AND WE'RE GOING TO SEE WHAT YOU CAN CATCH FOR US TONIGHT!'

Dan laughed, shook his head, and took a sip of his beer. 'NOT HAPPENING, MY FRIEND.'

'COME ON DAN, WE JUST NEED YOU TO REEL THEM IN FOR US. MAKE THEM BLUSH. THAT'S ALL. WE WILL TAKE IT FROM THERE!'

'I THINK YOU WILL BE FINE MATE,' Dan slapped him on the back. 'GO FOR IT!' he yelled and pushed him encouragingly towards the group of bouncy targets. Dan watched amused as his friend, forces his way through the moving crowd, the others tag tailing behind him. Dan shot Toby a thumbs up and looked back over to the girl sat at the end of the bar. She was still there, enjoying her own private rave. He walked towards her with an ego full of confidence, he over exaggerated his strides as if he was in a music video.

'HI!' Jumped out a frightening red head, 'YOU'RE DAN HAYES!' She screamed.

'I AM, YES, THANK YOU FOR THE REMINDER!'

'I'M SALLY.' She continued, ignoring his sarcasm, 'COME MEET MY FRIENDS!' Sally went to grab his arm, but he pulled away quickly.

'SALLY, IT'S LOVELY TO MEET YOU, REALLY, BUT I HAVE TO GO!' Dan walked off leaving her standing open mouthed and disappointed.

The girl at the bar smiled at him as he approached her, 'I THINK YOU HAVE UPSET SOMEONE!' she smirked and nodded to the direction of the scolding red head glaring disapprovingly with folded arms.

He agreed. 'I'M SURE SHE WILL BE FINE,' he held out his hand. 'I'M DAN.'

'KARA,' she replied taking his hand, 'DO YOU WANT TO SIT DOWN?' She patted an empty stool beside her.

Dan sat down beside her and placed his bottle on the bar. When he looked towards her, he was met by her eyes, the lights from the music booth danced around in them, and they took him in with a smile.

Her laugh captivated him the moment her teasing giggles escaped her, he felt relaxed around her, like he could be himself. Her golden-brown hair framed her face perfectly, her hazel eyes had an amber hue to them which made them sparkle. If you gazed into them deep enough, you could feel them absorb any pain you had hidden away inside. Kara walked with a glow; she wore a very visible aura, she was kind, loving and no doubt one of the best things to have ever happened to him.

Being with him was never going to be easy. He hated that he could not control the slander she received from bitter and twisted followers. Dan would constantly put out a request via his social media accounts for them to be respectful, and if they had nothing nice to say, not to say anything. Some took that more as a challenge.

He could post a photo of the two of them, and it would always be the negative comments that were highlighted because of a keyboard war. She would chuckle as she read their comments … **Why is he even with her? … She's ugly … He could do so much better … He should be with me!** … He couldn't believe how well she dealt with it all, but it also worried him that one day a comment would push her away. The last straw was someone telling her to **just die**, so he decided the best way to protect her from these keyboard warriors and their toxic typing, was to threaten his followers, promising them that any negative comments towards Kara would result in them being blocked. Dan had always thought it would only be them he would need to protect her from, never himself. He could never see himself causing her any pain.

Some nights he watched her sleep, the ends of her mouth would turn up slightly, she looked so blissfully happy. He would brush her hair away from her face with his fingers and lightly kiss her forehead, he squirmed when she flinched, then he would slide back to his pillow, careful not to disturb her and rest his head back. If his eyes were heavy, he would force them open, just to keep checking she was still there before he could relax enough to sleep.

08 – Help Me Remember

Dan woke with a jolt to find Jed sat in the chair near his bed. Jed was quietly brushing his finger over the stubble on his chin, deep in thought. Dan thought whether he dare make a noise to draw attention to the fact that he was now awake? Before he could decide, Jed had already noticed. Dan tried to reach over to grab the jug of water the nurse had left for him but rescinded when a sharp pain stabbed him in the side. 'Ah, *shit*!' he cursed, gently returning his arm to his side.

Jed rolled his eyes, 'here,' he said, and got up from the chair and reluctantly poured water out of the jug into one of the plastic cups on the side table and held it out.

Dan reached out hesitantly.

'Oh, just take it, you saw me pour it. I've not laced it with anything have I! Dickhead.' Jed shoved the cup into his hand.

'Erm … thanks,' Dan muttered brushing away the drips trickling down his hand. He took a large gulp to rid his dry mouth. 'Couldn't pour me another, could you?' He smiled cheekily.

'Don't fucking push it, or the jug will be over your head.'

Dan raised his hands apologetically, 'Okay, okay.'

'Mum wants to see you.' Jed told him, 'no doubt to get both of your stories straight to spoon feed the police, you know they want to speak to you both don't you?'

'I had heard, yes… Where are you going with this?'

'I want to know what the fuck happened, and I want to hear the truth!'

'I can't tell you.' Dan shrugged.

'What do you mean you can't tell me, don't play your fucked up little games with me, not now!'

'Look, I don't remember what happened. Okay. I don't remember… I can't remember.'

'Well, that's fucking convenient, isn't it!' Jed snapped. 'That will make it easier for you and Mum to conjure up some random cock and bull story. Funny how neither of you are willing to tell me anything!'

'I can't tell you what I don't remember.' Dan said, 'all I can remember is that she was trying to take me somewhere and we argued, and then it just went black, that's all I remember.'

'It went black, ay?' Jed let a laugh escape through his nose, 'Should have known it would be a boozed-up outrage blamed blackout.' He said, shaking his head, 'I want to be there when you talk to Mum. She's not awake yet, I've not long been down to check on her.'

'Why do you need to be there?' Dan asked, 'what, don't you trust me to be in the same room as my own mother, think I'm going to go in to finish the job?'

Jed lunged at Dan, gripping him tightly by the throat. Dan grabbed Jed's wrists in a panic and tried to pull himself free. Jed loosened his grip and removed his hand leaving Dan gasping for air. 'You're a worthless piece of shit, you know that!' He spat, 'fucking worthless!' Jed pinned him again, tighter before shoving him hard into his pillow and released him. Jed snarled at him through gritted teeth watching Dan struggle to get his breath back.

'What … the fuck … is your problem?' Dan gasped in between deep inhales, rubbing his neck.

'Is everything okay in here?' A concerned nurse appeared through the door.

'All good here, aren't we Brother?'

Jed smiled at Dan and nudged him with his elbow prompting him to agree. Dan could only manage a nod.

'Silly bastard drank his water too fast!'

She hesitated a smile, 'I just thought you would like

to know your mother is awake, she has asked to see you, Mr Hayes, would you like me to take you down?'

'That's okay!' Jed jumped to his feet, 'I can take him, I'm going down to see her too.'

'Is that okay with you, Mr Hayes?' The nurse asked.

Dan looked at his brother and rolled his eyes, 'fine with me.'

The nurse smiled. 'That's fine, I will bring in a wheelchair for you, are you okay to wheel him down?' She asked Jed.

Jed nodded, 'not a problem.' He smiled.

'I can see it now; you crank open the doors to an *out of order* lift on the top floor and then happily roll me over the edge to my doom.' Dan joked, regretting the words almost instantly.

'Don't tempt me.'

The nurse returned with a wheelchair and helped him into it from the bed, he hadn't stood on his feet for a couple of days, so he was a bit unsteady. Jed took control of the handlebars behind him and pushed forward, 'Here, we go!' he taunted.

Ruth Hayes, their mother was sat up in her bed,

sipping water through a straw, she had tubes round her face, going up her nose. Her head was wrapped in bandages and covered her right eye. Small parts of bruising escaped round the edges, and the part of her face that was free from wrapping was puffy. Her arm was wrapped up tight against her chest. Dan hung his head and looked away.

'Not going to say hello to Mummy,' Jed mocked, breaking the silence.

Ruth turned her head slowly to them both. 'Hi, boys,' she whispered and tried to manage a smile.

Jed parked Dan by the side of the bed, directly in front of his mum, probably so that he had no choice but to look at her.

'Don't want you rolling away now, do we,' Jed sniggered as he stamped down on the brake, locking the wheels in position.

Jed smiled affectionately as he walked round the opposite side of the bed planting gentle kiss on Ruth's cheek, 'How are you feeling Mum?'

'I'm Okay love.' She patted Jed's hand and looked over towards Dan.

Dan cleared his throat. 'Hi, Mum,' he said still staring down to his feet.

'*Hi, Mum?*' Jed mimicked, 'Is that all you have to say to her, *not how are you Mum? are you okay?* or I'M SORRY FOR PUTTING YOU IN HOSPITAL!'

'Jed, please!' Ruth sighed, 'maybe you should leave us alone a minute.'

'Not a chance.' Jed snorted, 'there is no way I am leaving you alone with him!'

'Then please will you stop with the mockery!'

'*Okay.*' Jed sighed and sat down.

'Dan,' she said.

Dan looked up to his mother's gaze, his face stained with the tracks of his tears, 'yes?'

'It's okay,' she tried to reassure him. She pointed with her free hand at the bandages on her head, look at us, we match.' She attempted a giggle.

Dan managed a half smile, which vanished almost instantly, 'I'm s-s-sorry.' Dan stuttered, 'I don't remember what happened, was it me?' Dan scanned her eyes, hoping for some reassurance.

'It's, going to be fine.' Ruth told him, 'We'll tell the police an animal jumped out or something and I swerved to miss it and lost control of the car.'

'An animal, in the middle of the motorway ... on a roundabout? Could you not think of something a little less juvenile?' Jed laughed, 'they aren't going to believe that! If you are going to lie to the police, at least make it a good one.' Jed huffed. 'I want to know the truth, and I bet it starts with Dan drank this ...' He hissed at his brother.

'Jed, that's enough.' Ruth warned quietly, 'do you remember what happened Dan?'

Dan shook his head and continued to stare at his feet.

'Convenient.' Jed snarled.

'Jed!' Ruth warned again, 'I only remember snippets, it's very scrambled.' Ruth began. 'Jed, would you close the door?' Jed did as she asked and returned to his seat, shooting a dagger at Dan on his way back to his seat.

'Come on then, what did this *dick* do?'

'Jed!'

'I'm not apologising for that.'

Ruth turned to Dan, 'we got into the car, you had fallen asleep after about 5 minutes, which I was very grateful for, you slept for a good half an hour. When you woke up, you noticed we were still driving, you got angry,' she paused. 'Do you remember any of this?'

'I remember I was angry,' Dan confirmed. 'And I remember, shouting and screaming.'

'We argued. Hurtful things were said,' Ruth choked on her tears.

Dan went to apologise, and his mother held out her hand as soon as he opened his mouth to speak.

'It's not something I want to get into. I was turning at the roundabout and then I just saw your hand on the steering wheel, and then I heard a large bang sound and that's all I remember, everything went black after that.

'So, it was YOUR fault!' Jed roared throwing himself from his seat.

'Jed, please, he's been through enough!'

'HE has been through enough?! HE nearly fucking killed you!'

'Language!' Ruth cautioned, 'as far as the doctor is aware, I don't remember anything, but he said I am likely to regain some memory of the accident in time, but that's not something I will be telling the police.'

'I'd rather the police took him away and locked him up, someone in prison might give him the good slap that he deserves,' Jed laughed.

'Well, it's not your call, Jed. Now I've told you. I'm not going to be the mother who sends her son to prison; he needs to be here.'

'You can't be serious?' Jed's face fell in his hands. 'She won't want him now, not after all this. Would you trust him?'

'That's not your call either. Stay out of it Jed, please.'

Dan frowned at them both. Jed glared back at him narrow eyed, and his mother had a familiar smile painted on her face. It sent chills down his back. Dan decided not to ask what they were talking about.

Being less than satisfied with what he had heard, said his goodbyes to their mother and kissed her cheek again. He walked past Dan without saying a word.

'I want you to promise me something, Dan,' Ruth said when Jed closed the door behind him.

'Anything you want, I'll do!' He promised.

'Get some help, please. Whether you chose to go into rehab ... or ... maybe counselling would be a good idea. I'm sure the doctors haven't been sneaking you in any alcohol while you have been here.' She almost giggled, 'you have already started the journey, and I bet you haven't even realised it. So just promise me. You will speak to someone.'

She nodded at him implying that the only answer she wanted to hear, was *yes*.

She was right, he hadn't noticed. He'd been too worried about her. 'I promise.' He answered, 'love you, Mum.'

'I love you too, you big softy.' She smiled.

Dan went to ask her about the conversation she was having with Jed, but she started to yawn, and he thought he best leave her to get some rest. Ruth called a nurse for him with the touch of a button, and he was escorted back to his room. The nurse made awkward conversation like an uber driver on the way back to his room. She made sure he had a fresh jug of water, gave him his shot of painkillers, and a menu for lunch.

'Oh, before I forget, someone dropped something for you, I've left it by the side of your bed,' the nurse explained before she carried on with her other duties.

Dan nodded his thanks to her and inspected the box. He shot his painkillers with a chaser of water and wondered who it could be from. When he lifted the box, he noticed an envelope. His mother always taught him that if you receive a gift, you always start with the card. He opened the envelope and found a handwritten note.

Dan,

Keep this stone close and hold it tight,

It offers peace; you know things will be alright

Amethyst relieves stress, dispels fear and rage,

It's held this power since the coming of age.

Amethyst is known as the symbol of sobriety,

It prevents intoxication and relieves your anxiety

X

There was no name on the note, just signed with a single kiss. He opened the small box. It housed a small purple stone. Dan picked it up and inspected it, and chuckled, *a stone? Really? A stone is going to keep me sober.* He chuckled again and rolled his eyes. He held it up a little higher and the stone illuminated in the daylight, it had beautiful inclusions of rainbows when he moved it round, he found it a little more fascinating than he thought he would. He read the note again, the handwriting looked familiar. *Someone cares*, he smiled and popped the stone back in the box.

09 – Dirty Laundry

'Dan Hayes?'

Dan turned his head to see a red headed woman cradling a clipboard creep hesitantly through the doorway, 'yes?'

'These are for you,' she said handing him a bag of grapes, 'I was always told never to visit someone in hospital empty handed.'

'That's kind, thank you,' Dan said placing the bag onto the side table. 'I'm *Sorry* … do I know you?' he asked.

'Well, no, not really … We have met once before though, briefly … a long time ago,' she cleared her throat, and shifted towards him offering her hand, 'my name is Sally, Sally Knight.

'We've met before?' He frowned at her, 'sorry, I don't recall.' He shook her hand and started the struggle back into his bed.

'It was a long time ago…' Sally smiled down at her feet, 'So, I run a column in, *First Glance* magazine, I was just … umm … wondering if you would be free to talk?'

Dan let out a deep wince as pulled himself onto to the edge of his bed.

'Sorry, do you need me to get you some help?' Sally asked.

'Nah, I got it, I'm good.'

'… so, you could answer a few questions for me?' she said, almost bouncing on the spot gripping a pen to the point her knuckles whitened.

'I guess so.' He sighed, suddenly feeling flutters in his stomach. He hadn't been 'interviewed' for years, but he felt flattered that someone would want to speak to him now when, well, he was nothing, he wasn't part of the world where flash photography and microphones followed you around daily. *This is the comeback; out of the rough*, he told himself. Dan shifted carefully to not aggravate his injuries, 'fire away.'

A little squeal of excitement slipped out of her as she reached into her bag and pulled out a digital recorder, 'do you mind?' she gestured towards the device. "Just so I can make sure I get everything?'

'I guess not.' Dan smiled as he tried to place her. *She must have been a fan, maybe? She could have had a meet and greet pass? That must be how I've met her before, that's why she looks familiar, she's a fan.*

'Great!' Sally almost jumped on the spot. She began to open her clipboard, which had a notepad stored inside, which he presumed had her questions in.

'You can take a seat you know, I don't bite,' Dan said as he offered the bedside chair.

'Oh, thank you,' Sally's cheeks blushed as she sat down, 'Okay, are you ready?

'Yep!' Dan replied as Sally pushed the record button.

'Right, so, Mr Hayes,' she beamed a wide smile.

'No, please call me Dan, Mr Hayes is a little too formal for me.'

'So, *Dan*. First, I would just like to say that I am so sorry to hear about the accident, how are you feeling?'

'I have felt better,' he managed a sound that slightly resembled a chuckle. 'Sorry I'm a bit bruised down this side, it's very tender here,' Dan answered, pointing to his ribs.

'It must have been pretty traumatising going through something like that.'

'One way to put it.'

'How did it happen?'

'… umm … I don't know … really …'

'Surely, you remember something?' Sally queried.

'Well, the knock on the head has prevented that … so … I'm sorry … why are you here exactly?

'Oh … sorry … of course, I didn't mean to pry,' Sally apologised awkwardly, 'I was curious …'

'… Right …' Dan replied warily.

'Umm... So, have you been told when you will be discharged?'

'Not yet.'

Sally cleared her throat, 'so, there has been a rumour circulating, and it would be great if you could clear something … you were in a relationship with Kara Wilson for a number of years, but I understand that that relationship has now come to an end?'

'Was that the question or are you stating a fact? Yes, the relationship is done.'

'Has Kara always had a close relationship with your brother?'

'Well, they have always been good friends in the sense that they get on well. They must still do I guess, why else would she come here with him?'

'She's been to visit you?'

'With my brother, yes.'

'So, they are together?'

'No … I didn't say that.'

She shot an awkward smile, '…umm … I'm sorry. There have been rumours to suggest that they are. would you care to comment on how you feel about their new relationship?'

'What?!' Dan growled, 'NO, I don't care to fucking comment!'

Sally raised her hands apologetically, dropping her pen, 'look … I'm sorry, I don't mean to intrude… I'm only given the questions to ask … I don't write them myself.' She explained as she reached down for her pen.

Dan rolled his eyes, 'no … its fine … sorry …' he sighed, 'it's none of my business what she does anymore … I lost that entitlement.'

'Do you miss her?' Sally asked.

'Seriously? What kind of question is that? Do I miss the love of my life? Of course, I do! Every bloody day.' He replied, *'so I pick up the bottle to forget, even though that's what drove her away in the first place.'* Dan muttered a little too loudly to himself. *Shit. I don't suppose she heard that …*

'Sorry … the bottle?' Sally asked, 'I didn't quite catch what you said …'

Oh … she heard alright … shit! Dan waved his hand, 'oh, nothing … it's nothing,'

'Okay … sorry I know this may be a bit of a delicate subject.'

'You could say that. Could we maybe change the subject?'

Sally gave a sympathetic nod, 'so, will be seeing a Danny Hayes comeback?'

'Most definitely!' Dan tried to sound more upbeat, 'I have been working on some new sounds... well before all this.'

'So, watch this space then?'

'Exactly.' Dan winced as a pain shot down his side, '… umm … sorry … I'm starting to get a bit uncomfortable; would you mind if we continued this another time?'

'Oh, sure … of course, sorry! We can rearrange,' She smiled, 'here, take my card, that has my details, but I'll be in touch. You make sure you get some rest.'

Sally quickly packed her belongings and cradled her

clipboard the same way she had when she walked into his room. She said a quick goodbye and scurried out of the door.

How the bloody hell would she be in touch? She has no way of contacting me, he laughed to himself. He let his head fall back onto his pillow, Sally's words dancing round his head. *Was Kara really with Jed, was that true? She wouldn't do that to me, would she?*

Dan cut off his self-destruction. He remembered how the journalists used to twist their own stories. It wouldn't be hard for this Sally person to cut and paste and rearrange words in a written article. She could type what the hell she wanted. Dan just didn't want people to believe it. He had already slipped up mentioning the bottle under his breath, but those digital recorders can pick up *everything*. *Fuck it.*

'Well, there's nothing you can do about it now, Hayes,' he told the room. He would just have to wait for the article to be printed. Where the hell would he get a copy of this *First Glance Magazine*? He had never heard of it. Maybe one of the nurses would know. Things had changed. He was interviewed by the likes of *Smash Hits Magazine* back in the day, and it was a lot more glamorous. There was always a photo shoot either before or after the interview. *I wonder why Sally didn't take any photos? Odd,* he thought, the sight of me would give people something to gossip about.

'No matter what that article says, I'm still going to be branded the bad guy, I always am,' he said out loud. *Jed is going to be pissed.*

Dan let out a long sigh and pressed the buzzer beside his bed to put in an order for his medicinal cocktail, asking the nurse to wake him when it was shot time.

10 – Bottled Up Love

'Well, well, well, what a surprise that this ended up on the front page.' Jed turned the paper round to show Kara.

'Is that ... is that me?'

Jed frowned and turned it back to face him, 'oh, I didn't see that.'

'But I didn't have anything to do with that accident,' Kara said tossing the tea towel into the sink.

'I don't think it's to do with the crash, it's because you're linked to Dan, adds to the drama. You know what the media is like. You want me to read it and let you know what it says?'

Kara nodded and retrieved a now very damp tea towel from the sink, rang it out and placed it in the washing machine.

Jed sat quietly as he scanned through the paper. 'Well... um ...'

'Um? What's um? Jed what does it say?'

'How about we, skip the hospital visit and go out, get a coffee ... or some-'

'Jed!'

'Now, don't panic ... but this stirs up quite a speculation about the cause of the accident and how Dan might not be in his right mind.'

'Just tell me!'

'Well apparently, you've been trying to hide a pregnancy as a result of an affair ... with me.' Jed winked, 'and um ... Dan found out and went off the handle and tried to kill himself ... with our mother in the car? ... Really? I mean who makes this stuff up?' Jed said as he threw the paper to the floor.

'But we know that's not true, it was an accident. We knew he wouldn't react well being taken to rehab.'

Jed eyed her, 'but he did cause the crash that could have killed Mum, and himself. Bloody idiot.'

'Do you think he's seen this?'

'Seen it? I think he's the one that's dished the dirt!'

'Oh, don't be ridiculous, he wouldn't do that ... would he?'

'Are you worried about what he's going to think?'

'I wanted to tell him before a tabloid did, I didn't think they would even be an issue now! How did they even know?' *Maybe someone saw us leaving the clinic?* She thought to herself.

'Well, they have kind of saved you on that one,' Jed smirked as he tapped his finger over the article.

'I won't hide the fact that the baby is his, Jed.'

'And what kind of role model is he going to make?'

'You can argue your case all you like; my decision isn't up for debate.'

'Whatever Kara wants.' Jed huffed and stormed towards the door.

'Where are you going? We're supposed to be going to see your mum, I have the scan picture in my bag for her,' Kara called after him.

'I'm going out. You do as you please,' Jed replied coldly, slamming the door behind him.

Ruth had woken again with a fuzzy head, forgetting for a moment where she was, it was a recurring thing after a short nap. Her body gave her a warning jolt of pain each time she moved; she could feel every muscle pulsate. She pressed the button to summon a nurse.

'How are you feeling, Ms Hayes?' the nurse asked as she scanned the notes at the foot of her bed, 'I can see you are due your medication. I will get that for you.' She went to turn out of the door.

'No, wait,' she crocked, 'have the police been?'

'No, Ms Hayes, not yet' the nurse replied.

'Can I ask a favour?'

'Of course, what is it?' the nurse asked.

'When the Police get here, please send them to me first … not Dan … please?'

'I will leave a note with reception. I'll be back with your pain relief,' the nurse told her, greeting someone in the doorway as she left.

'Thank you.' Ruth smiled.

'Hi, Mrs Hayes.' Came a delicate voice.

Ruth looked up, 'Kara dear, how are you? … How many times have I have told you, call me Ruth.' She said giving her hand a squeeze.

'I'm fine, thank you, but I'm more worried about

you, how are you feeling?'

'A little squiffy, but I will get there, love.'

'You will indeed, I just thought I would pop and see you as, well … here.' Kara grinned as she handed Ruth a black and white image, 'it's only early days, yet, but things look good I'm told.'

'Oh … look … at … that little blob,' Ruth cooed, 'oh my gosh, how precious, can you believe that little thing will be a bouncing baby. It's just amazing.'

'You can keep that one, they gave me a few.'

'Oh, really, oh thank you love, I will cherish it. I really will. It will certainly brighten up my days in here … does Dan know yet?'

'No, he doesn't, I'm just not ready to tell him.'

'But you will tell him?'

'I will tell him.'

'Have you seen him today?'

'No … I haven't … I'm worried Jed has gone to see him though. You haven't seen the paper, have you?'

'No, I haven't ... why are you worried Jed's gone to see Dan?'

'Nothing, honestly, forget I said anything … anyway … I have to get a move on. I will visit soon. You take care Ruth.'

'Bye, Love.'

Ruth pulled the bed tray closer to her to reach her water and took a small sip through the straw and contemplated eating the strawberry jelly that was left from lunch. She looked at the sonogram Kara had given her and pressed it against her chest, this precious little speck gave her a warm flutter of hope.

'Are you out of your fucking mind?' Jed snarled red faced as he stormed into Dan's room lobbing a newspaper at him, 'who the bloody hell have you been talking to?'

'First off, … Ow! You *dick*, that fucking hurt … Second … what the hell are you talking about?'

'Read it.' Jed ordered.

Dan scanned the front page of the newspaper he was assaulted with and immediately saw his name, '*wow* you're right, that's a great picture of me, *Kara* looks great too, doesn't she? We were a stunning couple, don't you think?'

'Are you fucking kidding me, read the article, dickwad!'

'Touchy.' Dan teased, 'I'll just have to admire myself then,' he grinned.

Dan read through the article; his grin dropped, and his frown lines deepened as he finished each sentence…

Dan Hayes; Bottled-up Love

Dan Hayes has returned to headlines after several years of shying away from the spotlight.

Following his break-up with long-term girlfriend Kara Wilson, the, *Take me Back* singer confessed to seeking comfort at the *'bottom of a bottle'*, admitting that his drinking habits played a part in their separation, *'Every day, I pick up the bottle to forget, even though that's what drove her away in the first place.'*

Rumours have surfaced that Miss Wilson has found new love, after she was spotted with Jed Hayes, looking rather cosy; nothing like keeping it in the family!

Although we can't confirm when the couple officially got together, a close source has indicated that the relationship could have overlapped.

A little birdie also revealed the couple could be hiding another little secret as Kara stated that she had put on a little weight.

The fallen star and his mother were recently involved in a collision, details of which are yet to be confirmed. After admitting his personal battles, could Hayes have been driving under the influence? Both been admitted to hospital where they are receiving treatments for their injuries.

Written by Sally Knight

What the ...

'Who the fuck have you been speaking to?' Jed demanded.

'What makes you think I've said anything! There are loads of people that could have sold this story for a few quid.'

'Dan, the only people that knew you were in a crash were you, Mum, me and Kara, unless you sent a group text from your phone before you passed out, you're the only one that has anything to gain from this!"

'The media always finds a way ... Actually ... it was on the news that I was in here ... What the hell would I gain from selling a story like this?'

'Oh, don't give me that, we all know your desperate to get back in the spotlight.'

Dan rolled his eyes, 'I don't think this article paints me in the most favourable light, do you? So, your theory is wrong there. Cracking title though, I'll give her that, would make a great song.'

'Are you taking any of this seriously?'

'Yes, of course I am.'

'So, you're saying you haven't spoken to anyone ...

at all?'

'Look, it wasn't me. I haven't spoken to a newspaper.'

'Then who then?' Jed eyeballed him suspiciously.

'Well, if you must know, a woman from a magazine came yesterday, I've not been featured in a magazine for years, she was just asking how I was and-'

'Was her name, Sally Knight?'

Oh Shit! 'Erm… it could have been … rings a bell.'

'Dan… what does that say … there …' Jed pointed to the name under the article.

Sally Knight. He read to himself and looked up to his brother, offering half of an apologetic smile.

'You really are a fucking idiot!' Jed spat, 'imagine how Kara felt when she saw this.'

'She's seen it. How do you know?'

'Wouldn't you like to know?' Jed grinned and folded his arms across his chest.

'Oh, piss off Jed. You don't know anything.'

'I know more than you do.'

'Of course, you do Jed,' Dan sighed, 'I bet this has made your day, piggy backing off me to get in the paper, paints a great image of you, swooping in on your white horse just in the nick of time, finally getting the girl. Who is to say it wasn't you that's the 'little birdie' informative?'

Jed gritted his teeth and stepped towards him, 'Be careful what questions you ask Dan, you might not like the answers.'

'Is everything okay?' a nurse interrupted.

'Everything is just fine,' Jed said through a forced smile.

The nurse judged him silently with a side eye, 'just thought I'd let you know, Mr Hayes, the Doctor is making his rounds, there is a good chance you will be discharged today.' She smiled.

Dan thanked her and she left the room.

'Ooh aren't we a lucky boy … name back in the headlines, you can cruise out of here soon, fresh faced, strum out a "come back" and sign up to one of them shitty documentaries,' Jed perched next to him on his bed, painting this fairy-tale portrait with his arms, 'Oi, you could call it … "Steering towards the Spotlight!" … eh, what do you think?' Jed mocked as he jabbed an elbow into Dan's side, making him wince, 'oh, I'm so sorry, mate, did that hurt?' Jed sniggered.

'Y-e-s-s-s!' Dan wheezed through the stabbing pain.

'Ah, that sucks, mate.'

'Verbal wars aside Jed. Is there any truth in these sightings with you and Kara? You would tell me, right? I am still your brother.'

'We're only brothers on your terms, Dan, you haven't cast me in the role of your brother throughout this shit show, break a leg though, all the best.' Jed waved and left the room.

Dick, Dan mumbled under his breath. He skimmed over the article again, *Bottled-up Love, cheeky bitch*. He tossed the paper down on the floor, *no doubt he has gone to fill Mother in on my latest fuck up.*

A nurse tapped on the door again and came into his room hesitantly, 'Mr Hayes?'

'Yes?' Dan flashed a smile at her, he was starting to like this "Mr Hayes" formality.

'The police are here.'

'Have they spoken to my mother?' Dan asked.

The nurse shook her head.

Ruth had insisted to the hospital staff again that if the Police come by for statements, she needed to speak to them. That was the plan. When it was his turn to be questioned, all he needed to do was agree with the story his mother fed them. This wasn't a problem. All he had to do was stick to the plan. Just tell them that he didn't remember anything.

Over the years he had learned to perfect the look of bewilderment, but this time he found it a little more challenging with guilt clawing at him from inside, after all, it was *his* hand that was on the wheel.

Oh Shit!

11 – Here Comes The Sun

'Aw, there's my boy,' Ruth said as she struggled to sit herself upright, 'have they discharged you?'

'Yep, free as a bird,' Dan smiled. 'How are you feeling?'

'I've felt better, love. Have the police seen you?'

'Yeah, they came, questioned me and left.'

Ruth shook her head, 'I told them to send them to me first. It was my responsibility. I was driving the car. I was asleep when they came, I'm sorry.'

'You have nothing to be sorry about, Mum. My nurse told me they were keen to speak to me after reading a recent newspaper article.'

'A newspaper?'

'Just some disgruntled fan Mum, don't worry.'

'Oh, well what did they say?'

'Not much, trying to push me for the cause of the accident and I just said I couldn't remember. I asked if anyone else was hurt, but thankfully no one was. I'm not sure what will happen next, they said they will be in touch.'

'Well, if no one else was injured, they might drop it then?'

'I don't know how many times I can apologise Mum, but I'll keep doing it every day.'

'We're both fine, that's all that matters.'

Dan cleared his throat, 'when can you go home?'

'They haven't said, Love, I've got to have more blood tests at some point.'

'What? Why?'

'Nothing for you to worry about, okay?'

'Mum, I'm ...'

'Stop apologising, Daniel.'

'Sorry.'

'You're never too big to go across my knee you know.'

'Am I too big for a hug?'

'Never. Come here.'

Dan limped closer to her bed and leaned over, gently placing his arms round her. It was a strain on his back, trying to compensate his own weight, but it was worth it.

'Promise me something," Ruth said as she rubbed his arm.

'Again?' Dan chuckled, 'how many promises are you holding me to?'

'Cheeky git,' Ruth said tapping his arm.

'Go on, what do you want me to do?'

'Well, I just wanted to say no matter what happens, promise me you will find a way to forgive yourself, I know rehab was a hard no, but please do try a therapist, it could help? Anything is better than nothing. And I want you to know that I believe in you.'

Ah fresh air! Dan breathed it in deep desperate to clear the smell of the hospital embedded in his nose. He didn't want to end up back in there in a hurry. The hospital staff were very caring, but they were rushed off their feet. He wasn't sure if there were a lot of patients, he didn't see much outside of his room. It sad that a few of the nurses had asked to work extra hours, resorting to hiding behind a desk to stuff their faces with jelly babies. The ward sister had turned her back, but she didn't look the type to turn a blind eye.

Dan patted down his pockets to make sure he had a set of keys on him, he couldn't be sure if his mother had taken them or not when she bundled him into the car. Guilt leaned down on his shoulders, *all on you, mate*, it whispered to him.

Dan found his keys stuffed in his trouser pocket along with the small box with the magic stone that was going to keep him sober, he laughed to himself, *still, nice thought though*.

To his surprise, he found his phone. He didn't even remember picking it up or charging it. It was on silent but lit up in his hand, he swiped open his notifications, *1057 twitter notifications … what? I can't deal with this now*. The number kept climbing. He shut off his notifications and stuffed his phone back where he found it.

Dan finally made his way home with his mother's words on his mind. He wanted to do as he promised; *find help*. He *can* do it, because *she* believes he can, and because he owed it to her. He knew people who had gone into therapy in the past and it worked for them, maybe he could try that.

He unlocked his iPad, opened google and typed "*a therapist near me*" into the search bar. A long list of names appeared, among them was a Dr Christopher Anderson, who had great reviews, people seemed to speak very highly of him. Dan copied the number down and went over to his house phone, dialled the number, and waited anxiously for someone to answer. He was greeted by a chirpy woman on the other end of the phone, she asked for his details and what his availability was, which amused him. He chose a date and a time and just like that he had made the first step and had an appointment. Dan smiled as he heard his mother's voice in his head, *'see, that wasn't so hard, was it?'*

12 – Therapy

Dan was greeted again by the wide smile from the receptionist as he approached her desk. He gave his name, even though he was sure she would have remembered him and sat in the empty chair he was offered.

'Your 11 o'clock has arrived.' Dan overheard the receptionist say, 'should I offer him a drink?'

Dan, reached over for one of the magazines, just for something to do while he waited, he wasn't particularly interested in reading about the top *50 sexiest celebrities* or *10 beauty secrets they don't want you to know*, he rolled his eyes.

'Would you like a drink Mr Hayes?' The receptionist asked, her head peering over her desk.

Dan shook his head, 'no, I'm good, thank you.'

'No problem,' she replied, and disappeared back behind the desk and continued the task she had been disturbed from.

Dan shuffled around in his seat. He hated waiting, he listened to the racing clicks of the receptionist's keyboard which had a better rhythm than the faint elevator music. It was boring enough to send a stubborn toddler to sleep.

It always seemed like he was sat in reception for an hour, if not more before he was called in to Dr Anderson's office. Dan was sure he did it on purpose.

The reception phone rang, which was promptly answered by the receptionist, 'okay, thank you … Mr Hayes, you can make your way down to Dr Anderson now, he is in room two today.' She smiled with a blush.

She's a fan. He thanked the receptionist with a wink and made his way down to the heavy brown door which had a large number two on the front, the removable door plaque read *Dr Christopher Anderson PsyD*, he knocked loudly on the door and waited permission to enter.

'Come in!'

Dan opened the door and walked into the room.

'Hello, Mr Hayes, sorry for the wait, were you offered something to drink?'

Nothing that would have made that wait more enjoyable… 'No problem, yes your receptionist did offer me one, but I'm okay for now, thank you.'

'Just to confirm, Mr Hayes everything we discuss in this session is confidential.' Dr Anderson said that before every discussion they had, which Dan was relieved about. He often wondered whether he ever said too much. 'So, how are you doing today?' Dr Anderson asked as he ushered Dan over to the long chair in the centre of a cosy grey room, with black and charcoal furnishings. A large windowsill showcased a rather elegant potted plant, its long leaves curved out like a foliage waterfall. Dan thought it an odd place to put a plant. He chose to sit in a small black tub chair parked close by.

'I'm okay, I guess.' Dan muttered eventually.

'So, what would you like to discuss in this session?' Dr Anderson asked as he picked up a pad and pen.

'Do we really have to?' Dan moaned like a stroppy teenager. 'I don't think talking does much to be honest, seems a bit pointless.'

Dr Anderson pondered for a few minutes. 'Okay, that's a fair comment, you're right talking isn't for everyone, but if you don't mind me saying, this is your fourth session and you have made every appointment – it must be doing something?'

'I made a promise,' Dan replied. 'And I am going to try to keep it.'

'So, what would be helpful for you today, or we can carry on where we left off last week?'

Dan shrugged.

'Okay, I want to try something different if I may?

Tell me … if I could grant you three wishes – what would you wish for?'

Dan burst into a hyena laugh, 'oh come on doc, I'm not twelve!' He met Dr Anderson's poker face stare, raising his eyebrows with the faintest smirk.

'It's a helpful exercise and it could help lift the lid on something that you have buried deep. So, come on, give it a go, humour me …. Three wishes, what would they be?'

Dan slouched down and threw his head to the back of the chair, 'I don't get the point in this but, alright … I'll play.' Dan stared at the ceiling for a while before he spoke again.

Dr Anderson was sat, pen in hand, readily waiting.

'My mother's forgiveness… my career back … and that bastard brother of mine – I'd like to wipe that smug smirk off his face, I just wish he would make a mistake or fuck up – not make me look like the dick all the time.'

'Why do you feel you need your mother's forgiveness?' Dr Anderson asked, 'how would that make you feel?'

He shuffled awkwardly in his chair before replying. 'I've caused her a lot of grief over the years.'

'The car accident?' Dr Anderson recalled, as he

skimmed back through his notes.

'Well, yes, but not just that, I guess I caused problems before all that,' Dan adjusted himself again. 'She was the one who got my career off the ground when I was younger …. in that world … things started to go wrong. Maybe I was too young. Who knows.'

'So, what would her forgiveness bring you? If she said those words to you – how would that make you feel?'

'Better, I guess… I would be lifted free of this guilt weighing down on me. I hate myself for that car crash, I don't know why I …' *shut up Dan* … 'If I could go back – I'd let her take me to that clinic – hell I'd run in willingly.'

'And you still won't agree to a rehab facility?'

'I'm here, aren't I? This was the compromise.'

'How do you know she hasn't forgiven you?' Dr Anderson asked looking up from his notes.

'I haven't really spoken to her properly since she left the hospital. My brother has had her stay with him since she was discharged. He won't let me anywhere near.'

'But you have spoken to her?'

'Yeah, I managed to see her when we were both in hospital, we spoke a few times, but my brother just had to be there to oversee one conversation, but he did leave after he heard what he wanted.'

'And what was said with your mother?' Dr Anderson asked in between his note making.

'She wanted me to sort myself out, get help – she told me she loved me before I left,' Dan went quiet has he tried to breath away the ache crushing him from the inside. 'But I never asked her if she had forgiven me. Maybe I should have.' Dan quickly wiped a stray tear with the back of his hand.

'It's not a weakness to let emotions take over.' Dr Anderson assured him.

'That's what got me in this mess – emotions.' Dan let out a long sigh, 'if I could turn the clocks back...'

'You hold a lot of regret towards your past actions – but the past is where they are – the reality is that we can't change that. The future however, we can change. You just need to take that first step.'

Dan stared at the ceiling; he already figured that it was down to him to make amends.

'And what about your brother? why would you see him fail?'

Dan's lips tensed; he could feel the anger pushing

through his hands and pulling them into a tight fist.

'He's the first to place blame on me – even as kids – I was the one who broke Mum's new vase, when it was him throwing the ball – but I was meant to catch it.' Dan chuckled at how ridiculous that sounded out loud. 'My brother has everything, career, money, Mum worships the ground he walks on … He never puts a foot wrong in her eyes – he paid for her rehab all those years ago – she seems to think we all owe him something. I certainly don't. He's even got Kara eating out the palm of his hand.'

'Kara … your ex-girlfriend?' Dr Anderson flicked back through notes.

'She's the one, well I thought she was.'

'Do you have a bad relationship with your brother?' Dr Anderson asked curiously.

'Well, yeah, he's a dick.'

'Surely, there was a time when you got along. Happier times?'

Dan shrugged, 'I suppose there were happier times… way back when.'

'Do you want to tell me about them?'

'Not really.'

Dr Anderson looked at the timer sat on top of a small coffee table beside him. 'We are coming up to the end of today's session, is there anything else you wish to discuss?'

Dan sat up slightly, 'well yeah, like I said earlier – what is all this for? All seems to be pointless chatter'.

'You are quite obviously holding on to some resentment towards your brother – guilt over your mother. We're going to try and get to the root and work through it. That will hopefully, in turn assist in building those relationships back up. If that's what you want of course.'

Was that what I wanted? He thought to himself. There was a time when Dan and his brother shared a strong bond – happier times – but was that something he missed?

Dan left Dr Anderson's office with a pounding head *what a bloody waste of time.* He rubbed at the tension in his neck as he glanced around. His eyes were drawn to a familiar green and white symbol. *Ah coffee! Why not?!* He thought as he wandered over the road.

13 – Why Did You Go

Dan ordered a large black coffee and found a small table by the window. He inhaled the aroma deep into his lungs, it had been a long time since he had been in this place. He had never been here alone though; this was a first.

Dan scanned the room, the clinks of crockery echoed in the background. People were chatting amongst themselves. No one had given him a second look. Before, there would be a small group of girls giggling behind him, sneaking a few pictures to post on social media *OMG!!! Look who's here!!!*

Now, nobody cared he was sat in here; they didn't care that he was alone. Even with his face fresh in the headlines, they just weren't interested. They were getting on with their lives sharing happy news with friends, shoving phones in each other's faces – he didn't have any happy news – or friends for that. He was alone. He couldn't even visit his mother, not right now any way … he couldn't bring himself to, that and Jed banned him from his house.

He hadn't realised he was humming a tune to himself until a girl walked past collecting empty mugs made a comment.

'That's a catchy tune, did you write that?'

'Umm, sorry what?'

'The tune you are humming, is it one of yours?'

'Oh!' Dan laughed, 'sorry I wasn't aware I was humming anything… just something that popped into my head.'

'Well, it sounded nice, maybe you should run with it?' She said as she walked back to the counter, flashing him a smile.

Wait, did she recognise me?

He drummed his fingers on the table, humming along in his head and began to add in words to himself, *I sit in the coffee house, all alone, where we always used to go, and people look at me, they wonder where you are. Why did you go?* … he took a celebratory gulp from his coffee mug. That was the first melody that had escaped from him in years. Dan sat happily repeating the words to himself while he drank his coffee, keeping the tune in his head … *I think she recognised me…*

Dan jumped at the sound of a familiar giggle.

'Someone recognised you?'

He looked up to see her golden-brown hair bundled on the top of her head, with random strands messily framing her face. Kara smiled warmly as she took the seat opposite.

'I was hoping I would find you in here... didn't expect the singing… it sounded great … anyway … I think I owe you an explanation.'

Before he could swallow what remained in his mouth to speak, she already began to answer his question.

'I'm not with your brother, no need to panic.'

'What do you want Kara?' He asked, sounding a little more unpleasant than he meant to, 'sorry … I didn't mean that the way it came out, just a bit shocked to see you, here, sat in front of me… talking … smiling even. With that article still floating around, my head is pretty fucked.' He ran his hand over his head, his mind jumping to every scenario.

Kara stayed silent and started rummaging through her bag… *oh God, I bet she is moving in with him … oh shit, they're getting married, aren't they, now she's come to rub my face in it … oh God please don't hand me an invitation I couldn't handle…* She pulled out a white card, she exhaled nervously as she presented it to him on the table and opened it out flat. He stared at the black and white image, of a blurred alien.

'It's true?'

'I'm pregnant,' she announced it in a whisper, as if she were afraid of someone overhearing their conversation.

Anger filled his face red, he glared at the image, *why would she think I would want to see this? Is she playing some sort of sick joke? Is it payback? Flaunting an image in my face of a child she's going to have with my brother?*

'The baby is yours,' Kara told him.

It was as if she could hear the thoughts bounding around in his head.

'The baby is not your brother's, we aren't together, we never have been, he's just helping me, you never responded to the message I left you, the night I tried to get you to leave that party, I went to your family…'

'So why did you call him *honey* at the hospital?' He interrupted, 'you really expect me to believe you're not an item.'

Kara smiled awkwardly, and replied, 'okay so, that one was petty of me. You just, you hurt me so much, I just wanted to give you a taste of your own medicine.' She admitted, looking embarrassed.

'And to kick me while I was down?' Dan arched his brow, 'I suppose he was in on it too wasn't he, Jed I mean?' He said as he swirled the remainder of his coffee round in his mug, which was now stone cold.

'No, he had no idea. I had no idea I was going to say it, and I really don't think he noticed what I said.'

Dan laughed, 'oh don't give me that, he put his arm round you, of course he noticed'.

Kara sat quietly for a while and stared at the expression on his face trying desperately to read him, questioning the decision she had made to tell him the secret she had kept these last 3 months. She placed her hand gently over her swollen belly, holding on to every ounce of hope that she could to put her mind at ease. 'You don't believe me, do you? You don't believe the baby is yours.'

'Why did you leave me?' Dan asked rather abruptly, ignoring her question.

'Leave you? … At the hospital? We were told to-'

'No, not the hospital. Why did you *leave* me?'

Kara sat back in her chair, 'you don't remember, do you?'

Dan shook his head.

'You were so cold to me the night you left for that party; with those lunatics you called friends…'

'I remember that … and I'm sorry for the way I spoke to you – or didn't.'

'Do you remember me showing up?'

'Showing up where?'

'At that house party you went to.'

Dan shook his head again.

'Of course, you don't.' Kara rolled her eyes, 'you were well passed it by the time I got there. You could hardly stand up straight, you were slurring your words, God only knows what you had taken... You were a mess, and when I tried to ask you to come home you shoved me away ... Your friends were cheering when I left, one shouted something sarcastic at me, it was - *bye, darling!* Or something like that. I hate those apartments. Do you know how loud the hallways echo? It was embarrassing, I was sure one of the neighbours would come out.' Kara placed her hand over her swollen belly. 'I had just found out that day, I really wanted you to make the choice to come back home that night, and talk, like I asked, but ... you didn't,' Kara quickly dabbed the corners of her eyes with her fingers.

'I shoved you! ... and you were ... and you didn't say anything?' Dan held his head in his hands, 'you are probably going to be tired of hearing these words from me, but I am ... so sorry ... I mean it.'

Kara smiled, 'I went to see your mum, and ... I ...

umm ... I told her everything.'

He noticed her cheeks already flushing red, 'Please don't cry ... I hate seeing you cry.'

Kara tried to hide it with a wide smile, but the tears beat her to it, she quickly batted them off her face.

'I thought you were going to go mad about me talking to your mum. I felt awful that I told her before I told you. That's why they were so keen to get you help.'

'And I bet "they" included my bastard brother too. Dan slumped back into the chair and looked down at his mug, *the conversation that mum and Jed had at the hospital ... was this what it was ... it makes sense why mum would be so keen to stick her neck out on the line just to see that I made a better Dad than ours did*, he thought to himself. Dan looked up from his mug, 'I need a refill ... would you like anything?'

'A latte would be lovely ... but Decaf though, please.'

'One Decaf Latte it is,' Dan said as he lifted himself up from his chair and made his way over to the counter. He stopped in his track, and swooped round on his heels to face her, 'you *will* still be here when I get bring the coffees back, won't you?'

Kara laughed and nodded, 'of course I will'.

Kara held her hand over her chest as she breathed the bitterly cold sharpness of the British evening breeze. *Why was he being like this?* She glanced her eyes towards the street, people were staring strangely at the hysterical woman almost falling into a curled-up mess. She straightened herself up and brushed the tears off her blotchy face. Not one person asked if she was okay, not that she wanted them to, although she overheard subtle whispers from two young women walking by, *'oh bless her, I hope she is okay.'* Kara fumbled through her bag for her phone and flicked through her contacts. Her fingers hovered over *Ruth Hayes*, Dan's mother. Ruth didn't live far from here ... Kara placed her phone back into her bag and turned sharply towards her destination. *It's not just the two of us anymore*, she told herself.

Ruth opened the door within seconds of Kara's delicate knock.

'Oh, what a lovely surprise, come in dear, come in, come in.' Ruth ushered her into the hallway, 'is Dan with you, it's been such a long time since-' her smile disappeared. 'Oh lovey, what's wrong?' Ruth pulled her into a comforting embrace, 'come on, I'll get the kettle on, we will have a lovely cup of tea and you can tell me what on earth has made that beautiful face of yours look so sad.' Ruth gave her a tight squeeze as she led Kara into the kitchen.

Kara sat quietly at the kitchen table. The kettle had finished its violent bubble. Ruth poured out two cups, 'there,' she said. 'I'll let that brew for a couple of minutes,' Ruth placed a roll of kitchen paper on the table. 'Sorry, that's all I have at hand … I best get the milk, ooh and biscuits, yes? Of course, biscuits!'

Ruth placed a small biscuit tin in the middle of the table and pushed it closer, encouraging Kara to take one, then went to add milk to the perfectly brewed teas and carried them over to the table. She gave one to Kara and she sat down.

Kara thanked her and cradled the cup to warm her hands.

'What's happened love?' Ruth asked, 'you must want me to know, or you wouldn't have come.'

'Mother, Dearest!' came a loud bellow from behind them both, following a hard slam of the front door, 'oops, sorry!'

Ruth rolled her eyes, 'honestly, Jed that door is going to fly off its hinges one of these days.'

'I said, sorry!' Jed protested as he appeared through the kitchen door. 'Oh, Kara! Hi! How are you?'

She looked up at him with teary eyes.

'Oh shit, what the hell has *he* done now?'

'Why do you always assume Dan has done something?' Ruth snapped.

'Mum, Dan has always done something, you just never want to see it.'

'Oh, stop it. He's a good boy.'

Kara fell into her hands and sobbed. Jed settled quickly into the chair beside her and offered her his arm.

Jed looked over to his mother, 'you really think she would be like this if it wasn't something he had done?'

They both looked helplessly at Kara as she tried to control herself.

Ruth grabbed the kitchen roll and offered it to Kara to wipe her face.

'I'm not even sure I should be telling you both this.' She revealed a white stick from her pocket and stared at it with a smile.

'Oh my God!'

'You're … is it positive?' Ruth asked.

Kara nodded gently, 'I thought it would be enough.'

'Oh, how wonderful!' Ruth squealed, 'what do you mean … enough?' Ruth looked at her puzzled.

'Has he kicked you out?' Jed accused angrily, 'I'll bloody kill him, see Mum, a good boy, is he? He's no bloody good, he's turned his back on the apparent love of his life and now his own baby! Proud, are you?'

Kara shook her head quickly in Dan's defence, 'no, he doesn't know yet Jed. There were so many people at that place, shouting, the music was so loud … and he was …' she trailed off.

'He was what Love?'

'He was completely out of it,' Kara sobbed, falling back into the mass of crumpled kitchen roll in her hands, 'I have never seen him that bad before'.

'He's still drinking, isn't he?' Jed assumed.

'He's never been like that before; I was sure he had taken something dodgy.' Kara sniffed and wiped her nose, 'he wasn't acting like himself. He even shoved me out of the way. He's never put his hands on me.'

Jed found his hands forming an angry fist, 'did he hit you?'

'JED!' Ruth spat, 'he wouldn't hit her, he didn't hit you, did he Kara! Tell him!'

Kara shook her head, 'No, no, he didn't hit me, I don't think he would have been capable.' She attempted a reassuring smile.

The room fell silent. Jed was irritatingly tapping the top of the table. His first thought was to go wherever the hell his brother was, give him a good slap about, and then drag his arse back here, and maybe slap him again. He knew his mother wouldn't approve that plan, so he continued to tap his fingers on the table while he thought of something else.

'How long has this been going on?' Jed asked abruptly, making Kara and Ruth jump in their seats.

Kara shrugged, 'I don't know how long exactly, I've only noticed a significant change in the last few months, ever since he got in touch with one of his old band mates. Tony, or Toby or something, I don't even know what his name is, I have never been keen on him, and I think the feeling's mutual.'

'I know who you mean. Well, that explains a lot then, he's a dodgy bastard.' Jed agreed, 'care to offer your infinite wisdom Mother?'

'Sorry - what?' she said drawing herself out of a daze, 'I'm sorry I just can't get my head around this… This is all my fault; he's going down the same path I took'.

'I really don't think he's on the same path Mother, your problem was different, you drank to cope with an idiot, he drinks because he is one!'

Ruth ignored him, 'Maybe, he's just worried about being a father, it does that to some people you know. You put so much pressure on yourself to be a good parent, even before the baby has arrived. It can send people off the rails, it can!'

Jed stared wide eyed, 'Mum … have you even been listening? Dan doesn't know about the baby; Kara just said that.'

Ruth said nothing. Jed shook his head at her.

'Kara, what do you want us … or me … to do?' Jed asked.

'Dan needs help, I need him to get help … we need him to get help.' Kara rested her hand over her slightly bloated belly. 'I don't want the baby to grow up without him in their life, even if there is no longer a future for us, the baby deserves to have its daddy.'

Jed placed his hand on her shoulder, 'just know whatever happens, I will always be here for you, and for baby, whenever I am needed.' He gave her shoulder a squeeze and smiled, 'We will sort something,' Jed promised, 'so, when is baby due?'

Dan returned to the table with her decaf latte and his refill of black coffee, 'still here! That is a good sign, thanks for not doing a disappearing act on me, although I wouldn't blame you if you did.'

Kara giggled a 'thank you' as he placed a steamy glass mug in front of her,

Kara liked this version of him. This is who she met at the start; this was who she fell in love with. She wondered if this was who he would stay as or if Dan Mark Two was going to make a show of himself. She knew that he was new to recovery. He had been doing well, so far.

Whatever Ruth had said to him, she had got through that thick head of his. Maybe now he knew the truth about the baby, it would give him something to fight for. If he even wanted the baby, he hadn't said anything other than how sorry he was. Does she press him now …

wait a while? It was unknown territory for them both. *What if he couldn't handle the pressure of being a new dad? What if the baby was too much? I must know, am I doing this alone or is he coming along for the ride? I'll leave the sonogram on the table, open, in front of him, maybe point out baby's feet. Will he want to know what we are having?*

'… H-e-l-l-o-o! Earth to Kara …' Dan said waving his hands in front of her face.

'Oh sorry, I zoned out a minute there,'

'Is that a pregnancy thing or a *shit* how do I say I need to leave thing?' Dan joked.

Kara smiled at the fact he had just referred to the pregnancy, 'I have started to go a little spacey … must be all the hormones.'

'… So, what happens now?' Dan asked.

Her phone vibrated, breaking her attention as she was about to answer him. Kara's face changed as she looked at her screen.

'Saved by the bell? Or buzz in this case?'

'Oh no,' she giggled awkwardly, 'erm … I'm so sorry I have to go.' Kara forced an "everything is fine smile", 'I'm so sorry, I've just wasted the coffee you got for me.'

'Wait a sec, I'll ask them for a takeaway cup,' Dan said making his way over to the till again.

Kara watched as the young blonde tilted her head to the side while Dan made charming small talk, asking for a disposable cup for his "friend" so she could take her coffee with her.

'Thank you gorgeous, appreciate it.'

The young girl blushed as he walked back to his table.

'There you go madame, one disposable coffee cup.'

'I see you haven't lost your touch,' Kara said, nodding towards the young blonde, who was still peering over at Dan through her bangs.

'What?'

'Nothing, it doesn't matter.'

'Kara, please, what have I done?'

'It's nothing honestly, its none of my business, you're free to see whoever you want.'

'You think I asked her out?'

'No, I ... I don't know, anyway like I said, none of my business, you're single ... I'm ... really needing to go now so … we will talk soon, okay? Oh, here, you can keep this.' She said, handing him a picture of the sonogram.

'Ring me if you need anything?' Dan called after her as she scurried out of the door.

He watched her and saw her answer the phone. She was smiling as she walked by the window, she peered through and waved quickly to him, she looked a little flustered. Whoever was on the other end of the phone was evidently someone important to her.

Dan couldn't shake the feeling he had in the pit of his stomach, it niggled at him, something was off here. He shot up and headed for the door, he pulled his collar up to cover his neck and flicked his hood up over his head, *well this doesn't look dodgy at all*. He just caught sight of her disappearing round a corner, her slow waddle had given him a slight advantage. Dan moved quickly to catch up, stopping at the corner and peered round. He noticed a black Land Rover pull up beside her.

Kara greeted the driver with a wide smile, as the car door opened. Dan moved close enough to hear their voices, *who is this guy?*

'Here you are, I didn't realise you had come so far into town, I would have given you a lift earlier if you had asked.' The man pulled her into his arms and planted a soft kiss on her forehead.

Kara smiled at him, 'I knew, you were busy. I am quite capable of looking after myself.'

'I've told you; you need anything at all, just ask ... Baby bump okay?' the man asked, rubbing his hand over her belly.

'Definitely a boy, got a right little kick on him.' He joked.

'Well, you must have like supernatural senses or something; I can't fell any kicking!' Kara giggled.

'Is there something wrong?' he asked as her smile faded.

'Must be the coffee.' she said, showing him the coffee cup in her hand.

'Ooh, has Mummy taken you out for coffee already, starting you young!' He said to her belly, 'with friends?' he asked her, as he looked round.

Dan felt fire as the man turned in his direction *that's ... my fucking brother!*

Hoping desperately that her smile was enough to disguise her guilt Kara nodded quickly at Jed, 'yes, an old friend.'

'She was with me, actually.' Dan said loudly as he

walked towards them both, he draped his arm over Kara's shoulders as soon as he reached her and flashed a smile at his brother, 'You alright there, Jed? You look like someone just flushed your goldfish down the toilet!'

'You were with him?' Jed asked Kara, ignoring Dan.

'She was,' Dan replied on her behalf, 'we had coffee just down the road there, it's okay, she's told me about the baby, *my* baby actually.' He beamed, gripping Kara's shoulder.

'You told him? … I thought you were waiting?'

Kara offered Jed a soft smile.

'Kara says you have been helping her a lot, through all this. I'm glad she had someone there for her, and I appreciate all your help but … hopefully you won't have to pick up the slack anymore … I want to be a part of … everything.' Dan shot him a curious smile, swapping his hand to Kara's opposite shoulder, and pulls her closer to him. He eyed his brother for his reaction.

Jed nodded, 'Right … okay …' He looked to Kara urging her to give him an explanation. When all she offered him was an apologetic shrug, Jed decided enough was enough. He grabbed her by the hand entwining his fingers with hers and tugged her gently towards him, pulling her from Dan's grasp, 'Listen, mate. You may be "Daddy-Sperm" but I will be the husband!'

'JED!' Kara yelled, 'Dan, we're not engaged. We're not!'

'So, he's joking? Bit of a cheap joke at my expense isn't it, Jed?'

'Well, yeah, that was, only because I haven't asked her yet.'

Kara squeezed her eyes shut.

'So, you are together?'

'Dan … I …' Kara tried to stutter an explanation.

'Do you not remember when I said to you, I would treat her better?' Jed smirked.

Dan huffed out a smile, 'Unbelievable.'

Kara watched Dan as he struggled with words that pierced through him like a bullet fired from a gun. He lost his footing momentarily, she almost reached out to steady him.

'You said … you two … this whole time?' Dan looked to Kara. 'You lied.' His voice broke and he started to back away from them. 'Is the baby even mine or did you lie about that too?'

'Yes, Dan the baby is yours. I swear to you.'

'That doesn't really mean shit now does it."

'No, Dan, wait please! ... Jed let go of me ... Danny! ...Jed let go! … Dan … Let me explain, please. Please don't leave like this … Dan!' she reached out for his hand to pull him back.

'Get the fuck away from me!' Dan growled. He pushed her arm away, a little harder than he meant to. Kara stumbled and lost her footing at the edge of the kerb. Jed jumped to her side and went to grab her hand, her fingers slipped through his, and she fell heavily onto the road.

Dan didn't look back, even when he heard Kara's helpless cries, or the curse words Jed kept firing at him. He kept walking, his anger leading him to the only place it knew where he could numb his pain. A place where he could make this all go away... *I need a drink.*

14 – He Got What He Deserved

Jed was supposed to be picking up an overnight bag for Kara. The hospital wanted to keep her in for observations. Instead, he was standing outside Dan's house consumed by a rage of "what ifs". He stormed in the front door, towards the blare of a distorted melody booming from speakers.

'Ohhereheis, the wannabe Daddee! ... come to take sumfin else from-e?' Dan slurred.

Jed prowled further into Dan's room. A dim light from the screen of a laptop highlighted a lump in the floor; Dan paralysed with whiskey, propped up against the side of his bed. If it was anyone else Jed could have felt a little sorry for him, but not after this. She could have lost the baby because of him. Anger brewed, fizzing through every vein. Devils' adrenaline rushed through his body.

'GET UP.' Jed growled.

Dan looked at him and laughed, almost losing his balance, 'Why?' Dan almost choked on his chuckles as he tipped the bottle towards his mouth.

Jed's phoned buzzed in his pocket, it illuminated the room as he took it out.

Kara Calling...

Dan sniggered to himself, 'Oooh, she'll do that a lot! Probably doesn't even need anyfin – jus "checking upon ya" in that very annoyingly carey way that she does.' Dan made wobbly quotation marks with his free hand in between hiccups.

Jed silenced the call and returned the phone to his pocket.

'Now… now that's… just gun get you in trouble.' Dan said smirking, 'sumfin I don't never have to deal with from her, and with hormones, shit, cheers bruv!' Dan raised his bottle at Jed and shot back another mouthful.

'She's at the hospital.' Jed grunted at him, 'somewhere I should be, now, *fuck* … JUST GET UP!' Jed lunged at him and pulled Dan up by the collar of his shirt and left him to balance himself on his unsteady feet.

'Heey! … You spilled my drink, dick! Dan whinged, staring at the trickle down his arm. He swayed on his feet. 'You wanna drink?' Dan offered the bottle to his brother, which shook in his unstable hands.

Jed drew back his fist, hesitantly as he battled his tugging conscience. Dan was to blame for putting their mother in hospital. Now Kara, only it wasn't Kara's life he could have put in danger.

'What if she loses the baby? *Your baby*, why don't

you care like I do?' Jed yelled.

Jed stared at the shaking bottle, and then to his brother, hoping to see some sort of remorse escape his eyes, but his eyes were glazed. His expression was smug.

Dan waited for him to accept his offering.

Indignation surged within him; Jed snatched the bottle from his brother's hand. Dan fell forward, as if he was still attached to his drink. With a home run swing, Jed struck Dan on the side of his head, shattering the bottle into sharp confetti. Dan dropped heavily to the floor.

Jed froze. Fragments of the bottle were embedded in his jacket sleeve, the neck of the bottle locked in a tight grip. He fell to his knees, the bottle top clinked beside him as it hit the floor. Jed stared at his brother, his breathing was shallow, his head was damp. Jed hoped it was just whiskey he was soaked in, but then he saw the blood dripping down his face. *Shit*.

'Dan?' Jed jumped forward to his side. Jed shook him gently, 'Dan? … *Shit*. I'm sorry! … But you know you deserved this right?' Jed's trembling hands pulled his phone out of his pocket, swiping the screen to revive it, he dialled nine, nine, nine … *Shit …What do I … how the hell do I explain this? …*

'Hello … hello? Can you help me? … Please? … My

brother … he's been attacked … no … he's not moving … his head is covered in blood … can you send someone … hurry … please!' Jed gave them Dan's address and hung up. He looked down at his brother again, 'I'm sorry, but you deserved it.'

Jed felt a throbbing in the palm of his hand, he looked down and saw the blood dripping down his fingers. *Oh shit*. He rushed to Dan's bathroom and bathed it in cold water. The cut was deep. He grabbed a fresh flannel from the bottom of Dan's cabinet and wrapped up his hand, *that will have to do*.

Jed didn't wait for the ambulance to arrive; he couldn't risk it. He couldn't think of a story quick enough. *Shit did I say help my brother?* Dan was that out of it he knew he wouldn't remember him being here, unless the paramedics told him? *Shit*. He couldn't think of that right now, he had to get back to the hospital.

'Where have you been? I was beginning to think I was going to be staying in these smelly things all night.' Kara pulled a face as she picked at her clothes.

'Sorry, I got held up. How are you feeling? Is

everything okay?'

'Yes, I'm fine, the baby is fine. Now I'm just waiting for the … What the hell have you done to your hand? Its bleeding!'

'Oh … erm … so I was hungry, while I was at home and erm … sliced it on a knife … making a sandwich.'

'So that's what held you up … food?'

'You know me!'

'Well, I'm glad you have sorted yourself out. I am bloody starving!'

'You've not eaten? I'll go get you something, there's a vending machine, just down the corridor.'

'Ah you know my weakness, but no, it's fine. You go and get that war wound looked at. The blood is making me feel queasy.'

'I tell you what, I will go to the raid the vending machine and then I'll go and get this mess sorted. I promise. Sound fair?'

'Okay. Just try not to cover anything in blood!'

Jed returned with a cheese and pickle sandwich, a mars bar and a packet of salt and vinegar crisps.

'Oh, thank you. You got this from a vending machine?'

'No, I found the café ... here one decaf latte. I'm not sure it will be Starbucks approved but it's the best I can offer in these circumstances.'

'Thank you, Jed, that's sweet of you ... right now go and get that hand looked at!'

'Yes Ma'am.'

Dan grumbled into consciousness and jumped at the sight of the paramedics, 'what ... who ... where am I?'

Daniel Hayes? Can you hear me?'

'Yeah ... I can hear you ... where am I?'

'You're in an ambulance on your way to hospital.'

'Why.'

'You have an injury to your head, it's going to need stitching.'

Dan frowned and felt around his head until he

found a sticky patch of hair. A sharp pain shot through his head. 'Oh *shit*,' he said, more to the sight of blood on his fingers than the pain.

'Do you remember what happened, Daniel?'

Yeah, I remember, he thought to himself, 'No,' he told the paramedic. Pain surge through his head, everything started to spin around him. A white film impaired his vision, before everything went black.

Dan tapped his fingers nervously over his knee and watched the busy employees dressed like they were ready for a day in court pace up and down the tiled hallway.

'Would you sit still!' Jed grumbled.

Dan cleared his throat, 'Sorry.'

'You need to pull yourself together if you ever want to work with these people. They won't place their confidence into people who don't have it in themselves!'

'How do you know all this? And how did you get someone to see me? You never said.'

'I interned here last year; Evans owed me a favour.'

'Why waste that on me?'

Jed shrugged, 'Because I think you have just as much potential as any other under-sixteen-year-old in this industry. All singing songs about relationship dilemmas they're too young to really understand.'

'Where's Mum?' Dan asked his eyes searched for her through the glass doors.

'She's probably still circling the car park for a corner space. She won't find one.' Jed chuckled, 'ah, speak of the devil.' He said knocking his elbow into Dan's shoulder.

'Absolutely outrageous!'

'What is Mother?' Jed smirked.

'That carpark! The spaces are too narrow! I've squeezed in-between two fords; they were smallest cars in there.'

Jed leaned into Dan and whispered, 'See I told you she wouldn't get a corner space.'

'Have you spoke to anyone yet?'

'Not yet.'

'Do they have a coffee machine round here?' Their mother, Ruth, looked around the open planned reception area.

Dan raised his eyebrows and tried to discretely cover his silly smile with his hand.

'I think there is one over there by the desk Mum.' Jed replied, and darted another elbow into Dan, this time aiming for his ribs.

'Ah, thank God!' Ruth said as she hurried over to the desk.

'What was that for?' Dan grunted, rubbing his side.

'You know what!'

'Wait? You know? ... Does Mum know *you* know?'

'Does she know *you know*?'

Dan shook his head, 'I don't think so.'

'Well let's keep it that way, shall we? At least for now, while I monitor things. Okay?'

Dan agreed, 'Okay.'

Hayes! It's great to see you!'

'Evans, how's it going? This is my mum, Ruth and

my little brother, Dan.'

'Dan the Man! Great to meet you! From what your brother has told us about you, it won't be long until the world is screaming the name, *Daniel Hayes*!'

'Daniel Hayes? ... Daniel Hayes?'

Dan jumped to his name and raised his hand.

'Hello Daniel, I'll take you through now and fix you up good as new.'

They wheeled Dan to the nurse, and she cleaned and stitched up the cut on his head.

'This is a nasty one, what happened?'

'No idea.' he lied. Maybe if he kept this quiet, Jed might call off this, *War of Alphas*. For the first time in a long while, he missed the relationship they had. He wanted his brother back...

15 - The Message Was Clear

Jed had done so much for him when he was younger. He looked out for him. Now it seems his allegiance had changed. Dan sat in his apartment glancing through pages of paperwork he received in a brown envelope, some skinny man with a clipboard asked him to sign for it at the door ten minutes ago. It's amazing how much information you can assume from a document, just by reading a handful of the words. This one spoke for itself.

Temporary Restraining Order

Dan was to stay away from Kara, his ex-girlfriend, who was carrying his baby, and his brother, Jed, the guy she has decided to shack up with to play happy families. But what really hit hard was the final name on the list, Ruth Hayes, his mother, the only support he seemed to have around him, was now gone.

'This is complete bullshit!' Dan shouted to the room, tossing the papers into the air. 'They've all turned their back on me! Making themselves out to be the bloody victims. I'm the victim here. Me!'

Dan heard the letter box tapping and creak open, *'Daniel...?'* a voice whispered.

'Hello?' Dan called back, thinking maybe he was

hearing things.

'*Open the door!!*' they muttered back.

Dan opened the door cautiously. A woman barged through it, wearing a thick black trench coat, an oversized bucket hat, a tartan scarf that covered half of her face, and sunglasses big enough to protect six eyes from the sun.

'Mum?' Dan let out half a laugh as she removed the shades, 'What the hell are you wearing?'

'Why do you think I'm dressed like this?' she asked as she quickly closed the door behind her, 'What the hell have you done to your face?' she gasped cupping his cheeks.

Wouldn't you like to know he thought to himself, 'Oh, nothing, I fell … Into the radiator, I think … Isn't this against the rules?' Dan said sarcastically as he wandered back into the kitchen.

Ruth noticed the paperwork scattered across the floor, 'Ah, you got it then? I wasn't sure … Are you Okay?'

'What the fuck, Mum?'

'Now, look before you start at me, I had no idea, honestly. I've just found out about it myself. I don't know what the bloody hell he was thinking!'

'Really, you didn't see him pulling something like this. Let's think about it shall we? He steals my girlfriend; he's been trying to do that one for years! Then they hide their seedy little relationship from me all this time. He wants to raise *my* baby with her? I find out, and I'm the *arsehole* for lashing out. Now what could he possibly use against me to help him get this *shit* on me? Ah yes, I'm a drunk who tried to off his mother by slamming her into a lorry, yes Judge, that will do it.'

'Daniel, please calm down. It's only temporary.' Ruth told him gently.

'Calm down? ... Temporary? It's not even bloody necessary! What danger am *I* to Kara? Well, they've been very helpful in answering that one for me ... I'm a loose *fucking* cannon? I think I can well and truly say goodbye to fatherhood now. Might as well make it easier for them and just bloody end it all. Let them two play happy families together with *my* kid, I'll just watch over from the clouds.' Dan shoved the paperwork with his foot and paced to the other side of the kitchen. He flung open the top cupboard and started rummaging through it.

'Please don't talk like that, Love. What about me? Your mother? What would I do without you?'

'Well, you would be safe to travel in your own car, Mother.'

'Daniel!'

'Sorry.'

'Look, I really shouldn't stay long, but please, stop looking for that bloody bottle!'

Dan froze.

'You don't need it.'

'Well, it's done me quite fine the last few days. What else do I have?'

'Oh, Daniel you haven't!'

'I couldn't fall into a bloody radiator sober, could I?'

'Right. Listen to me, you have me, you will always have me, it comes with the territory of being your mother, you can't get rid … well you can try,' she smirked at him.

Dan closed the cupboard door and turned his back to it. 'That was a bit dark for you, Mother!'

'And I'm still here.'

'More fool you, Mother.'

'You have Kara too, and a beautiful baby on the way, and Jed … well … Jed will come around, in time.'

'According to that *fucking* paperwork, everything you said is bollocks. That shit there tells me I have no one.'

'It was all done in anger, Love. It will blow over, I promise. I'll talk to him and get him to drop all this nonsense.'

Dan let out a sigh, 'You'd better go before someone reports back to Saint Jed, unless you want to see me thrown in prison?'

'I know I'm taking a risk being here!'

'Yeah, a risk for me, nothing will happen to you!' Dan rolled his eyes.

'You're my son. I'm still going to be here for you, no matter what. Just like you will be for your baby. I had nothing to do with that court order. I was horrified when I realised Jed had included me.'

'What am I supposed to do?'

'You have two choices, Love. You can wait it out, it's only a few months, prove to them you are more than what's written in there. Or you could carry on searching for that bottle, drink yourself into oblivion, retaliate and face losing everything, and there will be no coming back from that. If you don't do anything stupid, Jed won't have any grounds to extend it.'

Which will be what he wants from me. Retaliation. 'You think I can do it? Not fuck up, I mean?'

'I know you can. Why don't you book another session to speak to someone? That Dr Anderson? You said he wasn't too bad.' Ruth smiled as she replaced her oversized hat and sunglasses.

'Yeah, maybe.'

'I'll see you soon, Love.' she kissed him on the cheek and slipped out of the front door.

Dan closed the door behind her and watched through the security hole. Ruth stood outside ruffling through her bag then appeared to be writing a note.

A piece of paper fell through the letterbox:

You have a long journey ahead of you, but you will always have my support. No matter what.

You got this!

I love you

P.S. This message will self-destruct in 10 seconds.

Dan let out a chuckle. He peered back through the security hole, but she had gone. He took out his phone to send her a message but decided against it, he didn't want to give his brother any more ammunition. Instead, he walked through to the kitchen, flicked on the kettle and made a note on the whiteboard fixed to the front of his fridge to make another appointment with Dr Anderson.

He sat down with part of the paperwork he had picked up from the floor and read what allegations his brother had accused him of...

- Mr Hayes was intoxicated shouting abusive language outside the applicant's home.

Was I?

- Mr Hayes refused to leave the premises.

Wait, I think I remember this, he said to himself, *bastard had me arrested, well I think he did ... I woke up freezing cold, in the early hours of the morning in a dull grey, damp looking concrete room with heavy metal doors from what I do remember. Well, I think I came off worse that night!* He read further down...

- Mr Hayes was verbally abusive towards expectant mother, Miss Kara Wilson who the applicant has staying at his property.

That's a lie.

- Mr Hayes was psychically abusive towards Miss Kara Wilson which resulted in her being admitted to hospital.

Okay, this one makes me look bad. It wasn't like that. I had just found out about the two of them ... and a baby ... I only pushed her arm away from me so she couldn't grab me... I did hear her cry, but I thought that was because I wouldn't stay. Maybe I should have...

Dan flicked though the last few pages, *hmm ... that's funny no mention of him assaulting me with a bottle ... that wouldn't help his case though, would it? Jed doesn't think I remember it was him*, Dan chuckled to himself. *And I'm still talking to myself*, he threw the papers back to the floor. *I really could do with a drink now though.*

Drinking himself into a coma wasn't the best way to get a good night's sleep, but it was his favourite home remedy, one he had inherited from his mother. Dan would watch her when he was younger and often wonder why she would do it, why she would need to. Only now he understood. Negativity has many forms, and it can overwhelm the strongest of minds. Once it struck the right nerve it would claw its way through burying itself deep.

Finding reasons to drink was a skill Dan had perfected. He drank like he was trying to drown tiny demons living within him, they goaded him, "come on, is that all you got? That's barely enough to paddle in!" the party wasn't over until the last demon had hit the floor cold. Even then in their drunken drowse they would provoke the next shot.

He stretched out over his in bed, flat on his back, trying to slow the battering inside his chest with slow deep breaths. The advice the Doctor had offered on his last visit to hospital swirled round dizzily in his head. He was slowly poisoning himself. If he didn't stop now, it wouldn't matter who looked after Kara and the baby, he would just be a memory on a mantelpiece that they would refer to from time to time, 'such a shame you never knew him,' they will say as they rock the baby back and forth in front of his picture.

Jed wouldn't give him a second thought; he would probably place the picture face down as he walked by. With him out of the picture Kara would be fair game, he could take her and the baby and be praised for stepping up, the superhero mounted on a white steed ready to rescue the bereaved single mother. *Suppose I could haunt him, express my objection in the afterlife. That could be fun,* Dan chuckled to himself.

16 - Let's Start This Again

Dan arrived at Dr Anderson's office a little over 5 minutes early for his appointment, and to his surprise, Dr Anderson was in the foyer handing a file to his receptionist. He turned as Dan pushed open the glass door.

'Mr Hayes, a pleasure to see you again. I was surprised when you made another appointment, I thought I'd finally put you off … You can go straight through to room 2, Mr Hayes. Don't worry, I won't charge you for the extra 5 minutes … Brie, if you could have that typed up by 3.00pm? Thank you.' Dr Anderson said as he started to follow Dan through to his office.

The receptionist nodded and adjusted her headset.

'Take a seat, Mr Hayes.' Dr Anderson said as he came through the office door, 'so tell me, what brings you back, you didn't seem to keen last time we spoke.'

'Yeah, I wasn't planning on coming back to be honest, but I've hit a few *bumps* in the road, shall we say. My mother gave me a nudge to book this appointment.'

'So, tell me, what's happened to bring you back?'

'I spoke to Kara ... she's pregnant … she's with my brother now … my baby though, not Jed's … I started … drinking again … heavy, on the day I found out about them two, my brother smashed a bottle round my head, although he doesn't think I remember, 'cos I was absolutely wasted, I decided that I wasn't going to report it and then, get this, he gets a TRO out against me, I mean – what the hell? So yeah, lots to talk about Doc.'

Dr Anderson blinked a few times before speaking, 'Well that certainly is a lot to take in. Why don't we start from the beginning? Then we can investigate some strategies for you to work on. What do you want out of this?'

Dan sniggered, 'It would be nice to have a relationship with alcohol where I can enjoy the drink, savour it, and say yeah that was nice - time to go, as opposed to getting paralytic and blacking out. I don't want it to be an issue in other relationships I have. It's already cost me.'

'Fine, we can work on that, if you don't want to completely cut alcohol out of your life, there is no problem having a healthy relationship with alcohol, if you can control the urges that leads to these outbreaks of addiction, but I'm not saying that's what I recommend.'

'So, what would you recommend?'

'Sobriety. The biggest challenge is living with an addiction, the biggest reward is living with that and not letting temptation in.'

'So, do away with alcohol completely?'

'Mr Hayes drinking is what ended in you being issued with a restraining order, yes?'

'I suppose...'

'Let's try this, alcohol aside ... what is the most important thing that you think you could do?'

Dan thought for a moment, 'I want to prove I can be a good father; I want to be a part of that baby's life.'

'And where do you think alcohol plays a part in that?'

Dan frowned, 'well it doesn't.'

Dr Anderson smiled, 'I can refer you to some groups that may be beneficial, it's your decision, obviously.'

'I'm willing to take any advice, strategies or exercises you have Doc, hit me!'

Dan listened intently to Dr Anderson's advice and took it away with him, promising to return next week with and update on how he was putting strategies in place.

As Dan left Dr Anderson's office, he glanced over to the coffee shop across the road, taking his mind back to the last time he was here. The day Kara told him about the baby, the day he found out about Jed, the day everything went to shit. *Would it be a bad omen if I went in for a coffee … lightning doesn't strike twice … does it? … Fuck it,* he said to himself and made his way across the road.

'Hey, how's that song coming along?' the young blonde behind the counter asked.

Dan laughed as he thought back to his humming, 'it's a working progress.' He replied.

'It's a black coffee, right?'

'It is, great memory,' Dan smiled.

The young blonde blushed, 'that's £3.50, please.'

Dan handed tapped his debit card on the card machine.

'If you find a seat, I will bring it over to you.'

'What service, thank you sweetheart.'

Dan sat at the same table by the window, thinking about the last time he sat here as the café door swung open, startling him. He was relieved to see a young lady helping an elderly woman through the door. He smiled at them as they walked by him on their way to the counter.

'Here's your coffee, Dan … I mean, sir … sorry,' the young blonde babbled.

Dan smiled, 'it's okay, you can call me Dan... and your name is?'

'I'm Andrea, but most my friends call me Andie,' she smiled back.

'Well, *Andie*. Thank you very much for my coffee.'

Andrea blushed and made her way back behind the counter.

Dan tensed when he noticed a couple pointing at him and then whispering to one other, giggling, they were looking at something on their phone. Dan took his phone curiously out of his pocket and checked his notifications. *What the hell? I'm trending?* He had silenced twitter notifications since the accident, now it seems he's the topic of gossip *again*.

Dan tapped on a link that took him to an article...

Family takes out TRO against troubled Hayes

"Another awkward blow of bad luck for Dan Hayes following his accident earlier this year. The chart topper's older brother, Jed Hayes, has been granted a temporary restraining order against the star. A close source has revealed that the family have been increasingly concerned with Dan's alarming behaviour towards his ex-girlfriend, Kara Wilson. With Kara expecting their first baby, Jed Hayes felt he was left with no choice but to protect his family. We have reached out to representatives for Dan Hayes, who have refused to comment on the matter."

What the fuck? He rolled his eyes, *well thanks for that ... Sally Knight.* Dan threw his phone onto the table and took a large gulp of his coffee.

17 -Am I Ready?

A light tapping disturbed him mid-pour. Dan shot his eyes towards the annoyingly loud clock which hung off centre on the wall. *Its bloody 9.45! Who the hell is that at this time of night?* Dan huffed as if he was expecting someone to respond.

He unlocked the door and flung it open.

Ruth stood wearing a soft smile, 'Can I come in?'

'Sure,' Dan said and stepped aside.

'Sorry it's so late.' Ruth said as he closed the door after her. 'I thought I should let you know that Kara went into labour, Jed's with her.'

Dan rolled his eyes, 'Of course he is.'

'They are waiting a little while before they head over to the hospital.'

'You know there is this invention called the telephone, Mother. You shouldn't have bothered wasting your time.'

'I think you should be there too.'

'I really don't think that would be the best idea, would it Mother? Aren't you forgetting that little thing called a *restraining order*? I'm the last person Kara wants to see right now and probably the only person she's not allowed to be within fifty feet of.'

'Honestly, do you not open your mail. Jed had it revoked. I told you I'd sort it. Anyway, you're the father, you have as much right to be there as anyone.'

'Do they know you're here telling me all this?'

Dan knew the answer as soon as she turned to him. He turned his head away.

'What happened has happened, we can't change the past.' Ruth told him. She grabbed his face and forced him into an uncomfortable stare, 'but we change, set new paths for the future.'

'Who's having the therapy, Mother? Me or you?' Dan teased in a feeble attempt to change the subject.

'Cheeky sod.' Ruth laughed, slapping him playfully, 'but seriously, I think it's time you all wipe the slate clean, especially with the baby.'

Dan frowned at her, 'I'm no good for that baby Mum, they will be better off without me fucking up their life too.'

'That baby needs you!' Ruth assured him, 'and I think you need that baby in your life a little more than you are letting on.'

'I tried, Mum.'

'I know you did, Love. Look let's put the kettle on, eh? We have a bit of time.'

'Actually, I was in the middle of pouring myself a drink!' Dan let out a short laugh, but stopped at his mother's disapproving scowl, '… I guess tea would be a more sensible option.'

See, change *is* in you, it's a choice. You *will* get there.'

'Thank you, Doctor.'

'Oi, less cheek, more tea, you. Now, where are you hiding the biscuits these days?'

'Top left, Mother.'

Ruth's phone rang in her hand, Dan hadn't noticed she was holding it, she answered in a hurry.

'Hello? Jed? Is everything okay? … Oh wow, right. Moving quickly then, okay … yes, I will meet you there. Bye Love, bye!'

'Is Kara, alright?'

'They're leaving for the hospital now. Jed said to

meet him over there. We can have that tea first, to calm your nerves.' Ruth's face beamed; she was very much looking forward to being a grandmother.

'I don't think tea will cut it, Mother.'

'Well then, have a biscuit. One smothered in chocolate.'

'I would but you didn't get them out the cupboard. Too busy gassing on that phone.'

'Excuse you, my first grandchild is being born. I'm allowed.'

'Just drink your tea, Mother.'

Ruth swallowed her tea in loud continuous gulps.

'Bloody hell! That's red hot! Have you had steel pipes installed or something?'

'No. I'm a professional!' Ruth said proudly. A little squeal escaped her as she turned to Dan, 'are you ready?'

Dan swallowed hard, almost choking on the tea he forced down, *Am I ready?*

They arrived at the hospital and made their way to the maternity ward.

'Are you sure this is a good idea, Mother?'

'Why wouldn't it be?'

'You really need me to answer that one?'

'This is your baby. You need to be here.'

'But I wasn't invited to come. I don't want to add any more stress to the situation, especially for Kara.'

Ruth stopped in her tracks, 'I didn't think of that… The last thing Kara needs is you and Jed at each other's throats while she's pushing life into the world….'

'There's no saying the staff will even let us in.'

'You're the father, they have to let you in.'

'Not if Kara doesn't want me in there.'

Ruth thought for a moment, 'the café!'

'What?'

'We'll wait in the café; I'll text Jed to let him know I'm here if they need me and to let me know when the baby is born.'

'Better than your first plan, Mother.'

They ordered two cappuccinos and waited in the café. Ruth reminisced about what Dan was like when he was born.

'I wonder if the baby will be blonde like you.'

'My hair's more ... brown, isn't it?' Dan asked.

'Not when you were little, your hair was almost white! It was a lovely colour.'

Ruth's phone buzzed on the table. They looked at each other. Butterflies stirred in Dan's stomach turning him nauseous.

Ruth unlocked the screen.

'She's here!' Ruth gasped; tears immediately started falling down her face.

'She?'

'You have a little girl!'

Dan's chin trembled, 'a girl?' he squeezed his eyes tight in the hope it would stop the tears. He cleared his throat and smiled. Ruth jumped up from her seat and threw her arms around him.

'Congratulations!' Ruth cried.

Dan pulled in a lung of air and let it escape slowly, 'whoa ... I'm a ... dad...'

'Shall we go meet her?'

'Yes, I'm ready.'

18 – The Day I Held You

'You have got to be kidding me, Kara!' Jed groaned, 'Was it not bad enough that he was at the hospital? Uninvited! ... Are you okay with this? My mother didn't really give you a choice, just showing up with him like that.' He paced round the kitchen, stopping at the kettle, he tapped it to life, and grabbed two cups from the cupboard above, he assumed Kara would want one.

Kara seemed amused. Jed making tea was a rarity, 'Finally, you're picking up on my telepathic signals!' she laughed. 'It had to happen sooner or later!'

Jed shot her his "I'm not in the mood" stare and chucked tea bags into the cups.

Kara sighed, 'Look your mum is right, if she can forgive and forget, the least you can do is try. Neither of are innocent in all this.'

'I applied to have the bloody restraining order revoked didn't?'

'That shouldn't have been applied for in the first place.'

'Are you kidding me? He shoved you to the ground... you ended up in hospital.'

'And I was fine, so was the baby. Dan was upset.'

'And that makes it okay? I can't believe you're defending him! We don't need him, Kara.'

'Look, I know you don't like hearing it, but *he* is her father, she deserves to know who he is.'

Jed didn't answer, he was vigorously mixing the milk into the teas.

'Jed, you're making a mess! Is there anything left in those cups? Don't you dare hand me half a brew!'

'Oh, sorry,' he stopped and handed a cup to Kara.

They both turned their heads towards the front door as they heard the dainty tapping on the glass panel.

Jed sighed.

'I'll let them in then.' Kara said, storming out the kitchen.

'Oh Kara, I was beginning to wonder if you hadn't heard me, I didn't want to wake the baby.'

Kara smiled and showed them inside.

'Hi … these are for you.' An awkward Dan handed Kara a colourful bouquet.

'Oh,' she blushed. 'Thank you, Dan. They're beautiful.'

Kara led them both towards the kitchen. Jed had disappeared leaving his cup lonely on the countertop, 'she must be awake … I'll go check.' She placed the flowers in the sink and disappeared upstairs.

'Are you okay, Love?' Ruth whispered.

Dan nodded.

'Flowers were a lovely idea. Well done.'

They could hear Jed and Kara's muffled words, with a final hushing from Kara as they entered the kitchen. Jed had his arms folded with the look of a toddler who had just been told he couldn't have something.

'Look who's awake! … Say hi everybody!' Kara spoke in a high-pitched tone. 'Dan, would you like to hold her? You didn't get to at the hospital.'

Jed gave an uneasy glare as Kara placed the baby carefully in Dan's ready arms.

'There, you go to Daddy, sweetie … Watch her head.'

Dan stiffened instantly, 'I got her, I got her' he whispered.

'Dan, sit down with her before you drop her, or something.' Jed snapped.

'Jed!'

'What? It was just a *suggestion* …'

'I'm so sorry, Dan. Please ignore your brother.'

'I think I would prefer to sit down with her.'

'We can go into the living room?' Kara suggested.

Jed kept a close eye on Dan as he followed Kara and Ruth into the living room. Dan took the first seat he came to, with Jed not far behind him holding out his arms at Dan's unexpected manoeuvres.

'Tea anyone?' Kara asked cheerfully. She pulled at Jed's arm as she walked towards the kitchen. 'Jed!' Kara retraced her steps to usher him away. 'Give him a break, let him have some time with her.'

'I'll go see if they need help,' Ruth winked.

Dan watched the silent bundle staring sleepily at him as he rocked her in his arms, 'Uncle Jed doesn't like me very much. Does he? … Hey, should we try that rocking chair in the corner. Do you think we can make it?' Dan stood up slowly not taking his eyes off his daughter and carefully made his way to the corner chair. He lowered himself down, and began to rock them both gently, 'Ah, that's better, isn't it?'

He tickled his finger over her tiny knuckles and hummed the melody he had made up in the café, the day he found out about her.

'Oh, I knew she'd go back off.' Kara giggled, 'I've made you a cup of tea, shall I take her?'

'That's lovely thank you… and if you wouldn't mind, I'm scared to move again.' Dan joked.

'I noticed you switched seats, very daring indeed. I'll put her down in her Moses basket.'

Kara placed the tea she had made for him onto a small round coffee table by the rocking chair. She approached the sleeping bundle with caution. Their eyes met as she slowly lifted the baby out of Dan's soft embrace. Kara blushed a smile, breaking contact awkwardly.

'Come here little one.' Kara whispered and scooped her into her arms and placed her down into a wicker Moses basket in one effortless manoeuvre. 'Hopefully she will sleep long enough for one of us to finish our drinks.' She said to Dan, still rosy cheeked, 'Are you coming to join us in the kitchen?'

'Sure.'

Dan grabbed his tea from the table and followed Kara.

'Hey, Kara?'

'Yes?' she replied from the doorway.

'I didn't ask, what have you called her?'

Kara wandered towards him and stood by his side, 'At the moment I call her sweetie or sweet girl.'

'Very Hollywood,' Dan joked.

Kara giggled, 'I have a few I like, and I can't make up my mind. I wanted your opinion.'

'My opinion?'

'You're her daddy, why shouldn't you get a say?'

'I just assumed you and Jed would choose.'

'Absolutely not. His name suggestions have been ridiculous, every one of them was related to a bloody car … Tesla was one of them. A hard no.'

'What do you want to call her?'

'I like Lilly … Cora … and Emilia … but I think Cora sounds a bit weird with Hayes.'

'She's having my name?'

'Of course, she is.'

'She looks like an Emilia.' Dan said adoringly to Kara.

Kara smiled approvingly, 'Yea she does doesn't she … Welcome to the world Emilia Hayes.'

Dan glanced teary eyed at the gift he had been blessed with. He had spent the best part of his youth chasing a world he needed to be part of for something he didn't get anywhere else. At least that's what he thought up until now. The concerts, the cheers, the screams, the fans – he clung to them, that was how he sought affirmation. He needed that, he needed them, he needed the praise, the love.

He looked over the tiny bundle sleeping angelically in the white wicker Moses basket that was edged in fancy frills. He breathed in the aroma of fresh talc and lavender baby bath. How could someone so small immediately steal your life from under you.

In his head he imagined picking up his guitar and starting to strum, he sang her the story of how he met her mother, how he almost lost her and that she was the magic that brought them together. He praised her in his melody and gushed over how precious she was. From the moment she was born his world changed, he was no longer the centre of the universe - or the star of the show. That much was clear. This little bundle had taken centre stage in his heart, the spotlight now shone brightly over her. He would seek his own validation now, from the only ones who matter.

19 – How I Treated You

Dan sat laughing into the screen. His eyes flickered, scanning the comments that came in, choosing carefully which one he'd retaliate next.

SeriousSass: Full-grown man - acting like a toddler! Sad!

Hayes4Eva: @SeriousSass What's sad is your profile pic!

Saycheese89: Mate - you need help!

BritneyisBack: Is he alone?

LoobyLouLou40: This song takes me back!

Is he ok?

Iamknight: Back on the "meds" I see!

Hayes4Eva: @LoobyLouLou40 LOVE this song!

Dan snorted and took his whiskey glass, shaking it at the screen before taking it to his lips. He set his glass back down, picked up his guitar and ran his fingers heavily over the strings, sounding out a familiar tune.

A mixture of comments filtered through the live feed as he played. Suggestions that he was a one-hit wonder, finished, too old, battled with compliments on his hair, music, lyrics, offers of marriage.

He scoffed at his audience, 'idiots. The lot of ya,' and continued to strum, stopping abruptly at the sound of the door opening.

'Do you mind? I'm working! I told you not to disturb me!' Dan yelled as he picked up his glass to down the remains.

Kara froze.

'WELL? What do you want?'

'Um...' Kara fiddled with her fingers. 'I've made you dinner … I thought it would be nice to eat together,' she said her cheeks blushing.

'Did I say I was hungry? Get out Kara!' Dan snapped.

He grabbed the whiskey bottle and filled his glass, slurping round the rim to stop it overflowing.

'Kara, shut the *fucking* door!'

She stared at him long enough for him to notice the hurt in her eyes. He turned away coldly and picked up his guitar. Kara slowly made her way out of the door, closing it gently behind her, muffling his heavily strummed melody.

CherryBomb87: Seriously. What does she see in him?

Stace-See21: Wow! That's how he treats his girlfriend? Nice guy!

Hayes4Eva: @Stace-See21 Keep your nose out! He told her not to disturb him!

Stace-See21: @CherryBomb87 I know right!

SmileyKylie88: No one deserves that! She should leave him!

'All of you need to keep your noses out!' he set down his guitar and scrolled through the list of people that had joined the live feed, 'blocking you, *Serious Sass … seriously blocked* … and you … blocking you … bye *Cherry Bomb*!' He gave the screen a sarcastic wave, 'You know what … Fuck this shit.' Dan grumbled and slammed down the lid of his laptop, cutting them off. *What the fuck do they know.*

Dan returned his attention to his drink and leaned back in his office chair, dragging the tips of his shoes across the floor as he spun himself. Dan glared at the blank screen. *I'm still relevant, I'm still here. I'm still making music.*

Dan's stomach interrupted him as it gurgled loudly, reminding him that he had just refused a meal Kara had prepared. *Why did I go off like that?* His phone lit up a message he set down his drink to read it. Of course, it was Jed. Checking in. He must have been watching the live stream or spoken to Kara... Messages bounced back and forth in-between sips. In-between strums.

JED: Bro! U ok?

DAN: Not 2 bad.

JED: Not what it looked like. Jus caught the end of ur live. Wat up with u n Kara?

DAN: Nothin ... y?

JED: U were a bit harsh. She does a lot for u. U humiliated her. All for those freak zombie fans of urs!

DAN: Rang u to moan, yeah?

JED: Just sayin like it is.

DAN: Yeah, Right!

JED: U apologised?

DAN: Busy workin

JED: On what?! It's the same old shit u been strumming out 4 yrs.

DAN: Jealous?

JED: No chance.

DAN: U wish u had my life. U wish u had my girl.

JED: The Fuck is wrong with u?!

DAN: Admit it.

JED: I'd treat her better.

DAN: knew it.

JED: Sober up and re-watch the live bro, Laters.

Dick.

Dan's stomach growled long and deep, forcing him to venture downstairs, where a possible fight could be waiting for him.

He peered his head round the kitchen door. The room was silent, highlighted by the spotlights under the cabinets. He tiptoed over to the fridge and carefully pulled the door open.

'If you're hungry, that dinner I made for you is in

the microwave.' Kara flicked the main light on, foiling his shameful mission. She forced a short smile and left the room.

Dan held his head in his hands and made his way over to the microwave. Surf and turf. It was his favourite combination, and something Kara hated making as she couldn't stand the smell of prawns. He beeped a few buttons on the microwave and waited for his meal to warm through.

He made his way back up to the bedroom that he referred to as his office space, hoping he wasn't about to indulge in a plate of stomach cramps. He set it down at his desk and brought the whiskey over to finish off. *Maybe Jed had a point?* He thought as his tossed the glass back, *okay, that's enough of the drink... if I've just agreed to something Jed said, things must be bad.*

Dan sat cradling his bloated stomach. There was so much food on that plate, but it was so good he had to finish it. He took his plate down to the kitchen and loaded it into the dishwasher. He watched the door, expecting Kara to come through. She didn't trust him to load the dishwasher. She'd always watch him closely to make sure he had put the plate on the right rack or the knife and fork the right way up. This time she didn't.

The living room door was ajar, so he spied through

the gap. He could see the television was still on, some vampire rubbish she had tried to coax him into watching. Dan could see that Kara was curled up in a ball on the sofa. He made a bet with himself that she was asleep, so he creeped into the room.

She is asleep. He smiled at her. He pulled down the throw that hung over the back of the sofa, and gently placed it over her. He crouched down by her head and tucked away the hair that had fallen over her face. 'I'm sorry I'm such a dick,' he whispered and kissed her lightly on the forehead.

20 – She's Mine

When shameful reminders of his past resurfaced all Dan wanted to do was convince his family that he had changed.

Negativity had spread rapidly throughout his social media. More of his followers were turning on him. He knew he shouldn't, but he read through some of their hateful words…

INTERNETGIRL4EVA: Why is he never with that kid?

WILDBILL32: Is it even his?

AngelShimmer11: Deadbeat

CrazyCatLady21: Will she not let you see your kid?

NEEDMORECOFFEE00: not trusted to pick her up in the car I bet looool!

Hayes4Eva: @WILDBILL32 what a stupid comment!

AngelShimmer11: @NEEDMORECOFFEE00 LMFAO!!!! That's hilarious!!

They were demanding retaliation. Like everyone

else. They could only see the bad in him. The mistakes he made masked anything he'd achieved since.

Yes, he had done some terrible things, but he was working hard to make amends. The relationship with his mother was stronger than ever. It was a relief to him that after everything, he still had her on his side. He wouldn't have blamed her if she washed her hands of him. She was so certain that he had it in him to turn his life around. He wanted that too. He wanted to make her proud. He wanted to make his daughter proud. He didn't want to be one of those deadbeat dads with all the talk and no action.

He was happy with the progress he was making, and he believed he could keep it up. He had to. He made a silent promise to his daughter the night Kara went into labour that he wouldn't touch another drop of alcohol. He had kept that promise so far. Though temptation called on a regular basis, he did his best to slide the bar over to ignore.

Dan had to accept that his future with Kara was not going to be the fairy tale they had planned together. They had many conversations about children, marriage, whichever came first. He wanted that with her. He knew that the blame fell on him, he had pushed her away when she needed him most. This was his punishment.

Emilia's cries have never woken him in the early

hours of the night. He hadn't comforted her with a song while he made up her feed. He didn't get to take her out for walks or take her home each night like a normal father would. Instead, his heart would break every other day saying his goodbyes.

Jed would walk off smugly with her in his arms, like she was his to protect. Emilia would grow to share a bond with her uncle that she should have with her father. He was lucky if he managed to take a selfie with her. But again, Jed's sarcasm would spit, 'Oh, another one for your followers.' Dan had to find the strength to bite his tongue against the sneering remarks Jed made when he held his daughter. Jed wanted a reaction out of him, but he wasn't getting one. He wasn't giving Jed that satisfaction. *Take it on chin. Don't fuck this up*, he would tell himself.

Saint Jed wasn't as innocent as he makes himself out to be either. Dan thought that Jed would have shown him a little bit of gratitude for not telling the world about clubbing him round the head with a bottle. Maybe he should remind Jed. Dan could cause his own trouble if he really wanted to.

They would never be the brothers they were, that much was obvious. The thought of Jed with Kara pained him, but unlike his brother, Dan chose to be civil. Whatever their relationship was; if Kara was happy then that meant his daughter would be.

The fear of losing her too made him sick. Jealousy burned inside him. Why should Jed get to spend all this time with her? He should get that time. She wasn't Jed's daughter. It just didn't seem fair.

I've suffered enough. Emilia is my daughter. He can't have her too.

21 – Many Happy Returns

'Are you having a laugh?'

'Jed!' Ruth scorned him.

'What? I'm not about to play happy bloody families. Not with him.'

'You're being unreasonable.'

'How? If I don't want to go, I shouldn't be forced to.' He moaned, folding his arms across his chest like a toddler.

'Well, I'm going.' Kara chirped.

'You go then, I'll babysit. There that's my excuse. No sitter. Sorted.'

'She's coming with us. She's not missing her daddy's birthday.'

'Mum, please don't do your good bidding right now, it's not the time.'

Ruth shook her head and turned away from him, 'I should bang your bloody heads together!'

'I agree with your Mum, Jed. You're not being fair. You can't keep him away from her.'

'She's, my child.'

'She's Dan's child.' Ruth corrected him and narrowed her eyes.

Jed stood with his arms folded over his chest.

'Jed, I think it's time you gave Dan a chance, *we* have,' Kara smiled at Ruth, 'You're making things very difficult.'

'Whatever.' Jed grunted.

'Right, we need to get a move on! Kara, are you still okay to come and help me set up?' Ruth asked.

'Yes … let me just get Emilia's car seat-'

'I'll watch her …You go with my mum, and we'll meet you there.'

'Oh, are you sure?'

'Yes. Go.'

'Okay, thank you.' Kara said warmly as she noticed Jed mood change instantly.

'We will get a lot more done without this little munchkin distracting us, won't we?' Kara cooed at the Emilia.

'Come on then Love, let's get these decorations over to the restaurant before they give away our hired room.'

'They won't do that, you've paid already.' Kara chuckled, blowing Emilia a kiss as she skipped out of the front door.

Kara paced up and down the room flapping her hands.

'Kara, what's wrong?'

'He's not answering. He was meant to be here half hour ago,' Kara stressed checking the time on her watch. 'He's still not here!'

'Okay, it's fine, calm down, maybe he's driving? You don't want him answering the phone with Emilia in the car, do you?'

'No, I suppose not.'

'He'll be here, don't worry, maybe he's just … stuck in traffic? *Maybe*. There are road works all over the place around this area.' Dan smiled.

'I'm surprised *you* of all people are sticking up for him, it's refreshing actually, considering he is probably arriving late on purpose.'

'The thought did cross my mind. I am trying. It's still hard seeing you two together with ... *our* daughter.'

Kara offered an apologetic smile.

'Look, why don't I get you a drink, relax a little. He'll be here. He can't hate me that much surely.'

'I'll just try him one more time.'

A high pitch wailing in the back of the car pierced his ears, 'shush, baby it's okay, it's okay!'

Jed's phone lit up again, he tilted the screen towards him, *Kara* again, he tossed it back into the passenger seat.

'Won't be long Em, we *will* stop soon, I promise." He shushed her again as her screams escalated.

A sign for a service station quickly caught Jed's attention. It was only a few miles down the motorway. He stamped his foot down onto the accelerator as Emilia wailed over the revs. He checked the rear view and shushed gently at the blotchy red face that reflected in the baby mirror. Emilia's dummy was nestled just under her chin. *That should soothe her for a little while.* He undid his seatbelt and leaned himself back, stretching his arm round her car seat. He used the rear-view mirror so he could guide his hand to the dummy.

The blasting of a car horn startled his attention back to the road in front of him, he faced the rear of the car in front coming up fast and slammed his brakes so hard he swore he felt the soles of his feet burn against the brake pads. Jed held in his breath as he came closer to the back of the car in front just missing it by inches. They came to a stop.

The driver in front glared at him throwing his arms about and was probably shouting something along the lines of *what the fuck are you doing? You fucking idiot! Keep your eyes on the road!*

Exactly! what the *hell* was he doing? Jed held up his hand apologetically to whom he assumed was a man and sunk down into his seat. His heart was pounding out a cold sweat. He turned round quickly to look at Emilia in the back seat. To his relief he had managed to put the dummy back into her mouth, she had settled down and her damp eyes were drifting.

As the traffic started to move in front of him, he put the car back into gear and set off slowly. His phone buzzed again in the passenger seat. He leaned over to grab it and as he went to slide the bar over, a sharp blip of a siren alerted him to pull over to the side of the road. *Shit*.

Kara ran frantically to Dan and Ruth, 'Jed's been pulled over by the police, he wasn't coming here, he was going to take her!' she screamed.

'What?' Dan shot up.

'He's been arrested for erratic driving! Someone thought he was drunk! I need to get her. Can you take me?'

Dan nodded his head towards to the exit, 'Let's go get our daughter.'

They arrived at the police station. Kara rambled incoherently to the confused lady stood behind the front desk. Dan calmed her down and explained the situation. They were asked to take a seat.

'I can't believe he did this.' Kara said as she fell into the seat Dan had encouraged her towards.

'Come on, this is just Jed trying to bend boundaries. He can't have been thinking straight.'

'How are you being so calm about this?' Kara frowned at him as a cold chill ran down her arms.

'Are you cold? Here take this.'

'Thanks,' she said quietly as she pulled his jacket round her shoulders, 'but, you didn't answer my question.'

'Well flying off the handle isn't going to improve the situation, is it?'

Kara raised her brow in surprise, 'Wow, the Dan I knew no less than a year ago would have just completely flown off into an unhinged sack of rage. Mode set to kill!'

'Um, well, first of all, thank you for that,' Dan chuckled, 'but, I must admit, I do have a rather good therapist.' He shot her a familiar wink. He had that same twinkle in his eye the day they met.

'I'm happy that you're happy,' Kara placed her hand lightly on his knee. 'You are happy, aren't you?'

'I wouldn't exactly say I was overly ecstatic about this whole situation in particular; I didn't think I would be picking up my daughter up from the police station at such a young age! But... yeah, I'm happier.' Dan placed his hand over hers and gave it a gentle squeeze.

'This is all my fault. I should have just taken her with me and left Jed to sulk. I'm so sorry.' Kara moved her hand and turned away from him.

'This is not your fault.' Dan took back her hand, 'It's his.' He nodded his head towards the seething stares behind the double doors.

Kara ran towards the door and grabbed hold of the car seat. The startled officer almost snatched back until he realised Kara was the Mother.

'Oh, my sweet baby girl. Hi Princess, hi! Are you okay? Yeah?'

'Hello gorgeous girl!' Dan popped his head over Kara's shoulder, Emilia gave him a gummy squeal.

'Kara? ... I'm...'

Kara glared at Jed, silencing him.

'Don't you dare. Don't you even dare! I don't want to see you, listen to you, or spend another second in the same room as you. We. Us. Whatever was happening. Whatever you thought was happening. Whatever that sick little mind of yours wanted to happen. It's done.'

'Kara! Please!'

'No, Jed. No. I'm finished. I understand that you

have bonded with her and struggling with her not being yours, even though that would have been physically impossible, and you know exactly what that means, but I'll spare you the embarrassment. Taking her? Seriously? What were you going to do? Send me a postcode written in some cryptic code so I could come find you both and sail off into the sunset?'

'I wasn't thinking.'

'Oh, you were thinking alright. You were thinking of yourself.'

'I'm sorry!'

'Sorry will never be good enough!'

'Ma'am, we do need to ask if you intend to press charges against Mr Hayes?'

'Too right, I do!' Kara cried without hesitation.

'Kara, please!'

'Kara, are you sure about this?'

'YOU!' Jed's snarled. Rage erupted at the sound of Dan's voice, 'this is your fault! You just couldn't leave us alone. You couldn't stand the fact that Kara was finally happy! You fucked it all up!'

'Jed,' Dan eyed his brother with a mediated glare,

'I just wanted a relationship with my daughter. If you want someone to blame, get yourself a mirror, you fucked this one up on your own.'

'You aren't fit to be her father!' Jed spat.

'Says the guy standing in handcuffs.'

'Can I take her home?' Kara asked the officer clutching a notebook.

'Of course, ma'am, we'll arrange for a statement to be taken tomorrow. You get the little one home. Have a safe journey.'

She thanked him and started to fasten the baby back into her car seat. Dan walked over to offer a helping hand.

'It's okay, I've got her, thank you.' Kara blushed, 'can you give us a ride home?'

'Ready when you are.'

'You're leaving with him? What the hell Kara?' Jed charged forward desperately trying to free his hands, 'I'll kill you for this!' He growled.

'That's quite enough out of you Sir.' The officer said sternly and led a reluctant Jed back through the double doors.

Dan exhaled loudly, 'crazy bastard,' and led Kara and Emilia back to the car.

'Here, let me take her, you get in.'

'Are you sure?'

'You don't think I can secure the car seat properly, do you?' Dan smirked.

'Well, have you done it before?'

'Never really been given the opportunity before,' he replied as he lifted the car seat into position. 'Sorry, I didn't mean that-'

'No, it's okay. I suppose on some level, I deserved that.'

'No, you don't.' He assured her, 'Right, let's get you strapped in missy,' he told Emilia as he pulled the seatbelt out. He paused to examine the head of the car seat. 'Now, I'm guessing … this goes like … this way? No, not that way. This? No... *Ow*, that was my finger … How does this work?' He turned to Kara in defeat, 'maybe you could show me? Just to put your mind at ease that she is in there properly.'

'Sure,' she laughed, 'it's quite easy when you get the hang of it,' Kara got out the car and stepped in front of him. She took the seat belt from his hands meeting his eyes,

'Okay, so you pull the seatbelt all the way round, you see this bit here?'

Dan moved closer and tucked his chin over her shoulder.

'You hook the long side here, then the lap strap bit goes under these little groves on the side here, and then just clip it in the belt thingy, and pull at these to make sure they are nice and tight and ... done!' She turned proudly, 'did you get all that?'

'That was a marvellous demonstration, I have learned so much!' He teased cheekily.

'Don't take the piss! I won't show you next time, I'll just watch you struggle!'

'After that performance, I don't think I will have any trouble.'

'Charming, Mr Hayes.'

'I'm always charming!'

'I would usually be inclined to disagree on that one, no offence.'

'I know, I've been a dick...'

'Oh, no, I didn't mean it like that, I was joking! I'm sorry.' Kara interrupted him, 'you really have been amazing, tonight especially! I was half expecting you to swing for him. Lord knows I wanted to. Still debating.'

'Well, I didn't fancy a night in there with him to be honest with you.'

'I'm grateful you didn't do anything stupid! How else would I have got home!'

'I'm pretty sure someone would have arranged a lift for you.'

'You mean a police escort? Imagine the looks the neighbours would give me!'

'Probably the same looks they will give seeing me taking you home! I see them all the time peering at me through their blinds when I come to visit. Gossip mongers!' He chuckled.

'They are nosey.' Kara agreed.

'Come on, let's get this little one back.'

Kara nodded and hopped back into the passenger side. She didn't say much to Dan on the way home. He caught her staring at him a few times, she'd blush and quickly turn away.

What's happening here. She's giving me that look. Does she want me back?

22 – Cup of Tea

'It's going to be a bit weird staying in that house alone.' Kara sighed as Dan pulled into the driveway.

'You'll be fine, you'll be able to starfish without that big lump taking up most of the room,' Dan watched Kara's awkward reaction, 'I'll help you get little missy into the house.'

Dan made his way round to the back door opening it quietly, so he didn't disturb her peaceful slumber. Emilia flinched slightly as he unbelted her and pulled out the car seat. He carried her into the house placing her down on the floor in the living room, 'should I take her out?'

'If you're brave enough, her travel cot is set up in the living room, I challenge you to move her into there without waking her!'

'Interesting ... Is there a prize on offer if I succeed?'

'Yes, a cup of tea and one of these new chunky chocolate cookies.' She waved the pack at him.

'Challenge accepted.' Dan said rubbing his hands together. 'Right then little miss, let's go,' he whispered.

With his best victory walk he strode smugly back into the kitchen tossing a damp muslin square over his shoulder, 'That deserves at least two cookies.'

'No way, she went back down?'

'Yep.' Dan said, whipping the muslin square off his shoulder lowering himself into a bow.

'So, you'd like tea then?' Kara asked, trying to hide her amusement.

'Sure.' He said, pushing back the forbidden image of a glass of whiskey, glistening in condensation, the ringing of ice gently clinking around the glass echoed in his ears.

'Are you okay?'

'Um ...' *don't lie to her*... Dan let out a nervous laugh, 'actually, I was thinking I could use something a little stronger than tea, after tonight.'

'I can understand that, but as the responsible parents that we are ... We are just going to have to get tea drunk on PG Tips instead, I'm pretty sure that's how the cool kids do it anyway! And not to mention I would hate myself if this was the reason you fell off the wagon.'

'That wouldn't be your fault.'

'Really? Is it not my fault that you are both constantly at each other's throats?'

'Not really, he's always hated me.'

'No, he hasn't.'

'There has been a lot of evidence lately to suggests otherwise. Him taking you for a start.'

'Dan, Jed didn't … I didn't mean for things to ...'

'You don't owe me an explanation.' He stopped her, he wasn't ready to hear how she found her happily ever after with his brother.

'You never did let me apologise.' She smiled as she handed him his tea.

'You have never had anything to apologise for.' He took a swig, 'Ooh could you add a shot of sugar in this?'

Kara giggled, 'A *shot* of sugar, sure. You know all these references to alcohol is worrying me, perhaps you should stay here. Where I can keep an eye on you.' She teased as she mixed a generous spoonful of sugar into his tea.

Dan daydreamed as he sat taking swift gulps of his tea. He gazed living room door, where he had not long ago put his daughter down to nap. He would love to be the first person she saw when she woke up in the morning, *I could give her a bottle of milk in the morning; learn how to make a bottle a bottle of milk. I could pick out her outfit; probably choose the wrong one, just for her to threw up all over it.*

'Are you okay over there?'

'Would you mind if I stayed?' Dan asked.

'Of course not!'

Dan's spirit lifted. 'Give the neighbours something to talk about, won't it?' He winked.

'Won't it just! I'll go check on her soon, she'll be needing a nappy change, no doubt. Do you want to help bath her?'

'I'd love that.'

'Let's enjoy these first, there's no going back once we disturb it.'

'It? That's no way to talk about our daughter.'

'You don't know her like I do.'

'Ouch!'

'Oh, *damn it*, I'm sorry that was really-'

'It's alright, I have thick skin.' Dan teased.

23 - Sleepover

Loud thumps jumped Dan awake. He heard Kara's nimble foot race down the stairs towards the front door.

'Expecting someone?' Dan called as he stretched out, 'sounds like they are testing the hinges out on that door!' He rolled out slowly onto the floor from his makeshift bed on the sofa, landing on all fours. He groaned as he pushed himself to his feet, 'Ah my back!'

Kara peered her head round the door, 'Are you okay?'

'That sofa has killed my back! Who is that banging on the door?'

'I don't know,' she lowered her voice, 'I think they have gone now.'

Another several angry thuds followed.

'Nope, still there. Want me to answer it?'

'Do you mind?'

'How scary could they be?' he yawned and went to greet the angry visitor.

'Hi, can I help you?' Dan asked the red-faced bald man who was breathing like a bull about to charge.

'Is that your fucking car?'

Dan looked in the direction of a sternly pointed finger, 'Yes, it is ... Is there a problem?'

'Too right there is a fucking problem, it's parked on my drive!'

Dan examined the position of his car, 'hardly.'

'It is!' the man complained, 'this is the boundary, here! You see these *red* bricks down the middle? You are parked over them. Move it.'

'Alright, mate, calm down, I'll move it over now, okay?'

'Too right you will! Bloody cheek, you don't even live here. Where's Jed?'

'Jail.' Dan smirked.

'Oh and that *slut* is onto her next victim already, I'd get out now if I were you mate. That poor baby will never know who to call Dad, the number of blokes she's going through!'

'You wanna say that again?' Dan challenged him, adrenaline puffed up his chest.

'She's really done a number on you pal, hasn't she!' he said, cowering back.

'Dan ...' Kara now stood in the doorway with Emilia in her arms.

He turned to the bald man, 'This child has a father. I'm the *fucking* father. Now get the fuck off this property before I do something I'll regret.'

'Just move the fucking car, arsehole.' The man scurried through his back gate.

Dick.

'Thank you ... I've never liked him.'

'How much of that did you hear?'

'Enough.'

Dan pulled Kara into a tight embrace, Emilia squealed between them, 'you're not a slut.' He told her as he patted her gently on the back.

'This feels a bit patronising.'

'I'll always be here when you need me. I owe you both that.' He said, kissing her on the top of her head, 'Was that less patronising?'

Kara blushed and turned back into the house.

'Lovely neighbours, by the way, very friendly.'

24 – Is This Love Real?

Kara was captivated with this new person Dan had become. Especially after the stunt Jed had pulled, she was sure he would have been gifted a fat lip as soon as Dan laid eyes on him.

She was grateful that he didn't cause a scene on the drive. A few years back and an altercation like that would have ended with the crunching of a nasal bone. Whose nasal bone would have remained to be seen. Just imagine the embarrassment of Emilia's father rolling around with Mr Armitage, while the rest of the neighbourhood curtain twitchers watched from their well-positioned armchairs.

Kara glanced down at her watch; the police were due round to take statements soon. That made her nervous. Was she doing the right thing? Did Jed deserve this after everything he had done for her?

She couldn't help but grin like a Cheshire cat as she watched Dan crawling on the floor with their daughter blowing raspberries on her belly. Emilia squealed the most adorable little giggle. He was so good with her. It warmed her soul seeing them together.

Dan never really got to spend moments like this with his daughter. Jed would always interfere or overshadow him. Kara just wanted Jed to relax and accept the fact that Dan was Emilia's father, and he deserved to be a part of her life. Emilia deserved a relationship with Dan too.

Kara knew why Jed wasn't so keen on having him around. They had history. Dan was a threat. He was the absolute love of her life, and in every way still was. Her love for him never stopped. He would always hold a special place in her heart.

Jed would treat everything as a challenge, he needed to prove he was worth having around, he needed to show he was the best choice of the two of them, but deep down he knew the reality; he would still be second best.

She wished one hundred times over for this moment, just a normal family making memories. Maybe there was still a future for them after all? Maybe if she was honest with everyone from the start things wouldn't be quite so complicated. *Everything is ruined.*

The Police arrived just after two to take her statement, Dan stayed with Emilia in the front room continuing to make her giggle.

Kara showed the officers to the kitchen. She offered them a beverage and asked them to take a seat at the dining table. They didn't stay no longer than half an hour, they took brief notes about their day, whether Kara noticed anything strange about Jed's behaviour. She detailed their disagreement; Jed was obsessing over Emilia seeing her dad on his birthday.

'He told me to go ahead with his mother to help set up decorations and that he would stay home with the baby, Emilia and bring her later.'

'Did you have any reason to doubt him at the time?'

'Not at all.'

'So, you would say that you had a very trusting relationship?' The officer asked.

Relationship... 'We've always been great friends. He has done a lot for me.'

'And what happened when he failed to turn up with Emilia?'

'Well, I rang him, several times. He didn't answer. Dan suggested that he might be in traffic or just running late. So, I gave him the benefit of the doubt ... I waited. A while later I got a call from someone saying he had been arrested, and I just freaked out worrying where the hell my daughter was and then Dan, her dad, drove me to get her.'

'So, what is Jed's relationship to … Emilia?'

'Jed's her uncle.'

'I see. Now, if you could just check through your statement and I sign it at the bottom for me. And then we're all done.'

Kara scanned through the notes the officer had taken, making sure he had included everything. Deciding she was happy, she signed it.

'Thank you for your time, Miss Wilson. We will see ourselves out. Take Care.'

'Thank you, bye.'

Kara sat on her own to gather her thoughts. She knew that Jed would want to see her as soon as he was released. She couldn't see a way forward for them. Not after this. Although she was fond of Jed and she cared for him, she wasn't in love with him, and she knew that she never was, never could be, she felt awful for letting herself admit it, but she couldn't help it.

You can't help who you fall in love with. The truth was she wanted what was playing out in front of her. She longed for the three of them to be a proper family. Dan had always held her heart. It would always be him, but after everything, how does he feel about her?

25 – Never Enough

'Yes, okay... I understand ... that's fine. No. I don't want him to come here ... he can't just ...' Kara paced up and down the length of the kitchen counter.

'Are you alright?' Dan mouthed to her as he walked into the kitchen, wondering who she was shrieking at.

Kara shook her head at him, 'well, I understand that this is his house, but I live here too and I .... Well ... where else am I supposed to ... Okay. Yes, I suppose I'll have to. Thank you. Bye.' She dropped her head and pinched the bridge of her nose.

'What's happened now?'

'Jed's allowed home, they can't detain him longer than 24 hours apparently. They have cautioned him for now, he's not allowed anywhere near me or Emilia. So that means I can't stay here. I've got to leave.'

'Playing petty tactics now is he.' Dan rolled his eyes, 'He's expecting you to get out so he can come back here? He could have just gone to Mums.'

'Oh crap, I was supposed to call her back.'

'Don't worry about that, I'll speak to Mum. You start getting some bits together, you can both stay with me.'

'Won't that just be adding fuel to the fire?'

'She's my daughter, you're her mother. I meant what I said ... and if it happens to piss him off, well, happy coincidence!' He chuckled.

'Shall we go stay with Daddy?' she asked Emilia, 'Are you sure about this?'

'Absolutely. You go pack, I'll watch this little munchkin.' He said in between munching noises as he pretended to nibble on her toes.

Jed climbed out of the taxi, taking out his frustration on loose pieces of gravel as he slowly made his way up the drive, he hadn't slept all night. He tapped around his pockets for the front door key.

'Jed! O'right mate!'

Jed turned round, 'alright Norman.'

'What the hell happened? You look rough as shit!'

'Cheers, mate.' Jed snorted a laugh, 'It's been a long night. A long fucking night indeed.'

'Listen, mate you should know, Kara had some bloke here last night.'

'Oh?' Jed replied intriguingly.

'I had a bit of a ruck with him this morning, don't worry mate, I got your back.'

'Have you seen Kara today?' Jed asked.

'Yea, she … er … she left about an hour ago, with that bloke. Sorry Mate.'

'Of course, she did,' Jed muttered.

'This bloke said he was the kid's old man! You know him?'

'He's, my brother.' Jed sniggered.

'She cheated on you with your brother! Mate that's rough.'

Jed didn't bother to correct him. He just shrugged his shoulders.

'Listen mate, if you need anything just give me a shout, o'right?'

'Yea, thanks, Norman.'

Norman patted Jed on the shoulder and

disappeared into the side gate by his garage.

The house was still. The only proof of her presence had been left in the sink.

'Two cups, and two plates. Tea and breakfast, well she was pulling out all the stops, trying to impress him wasn't she. Could have washed them before she left. Suppose I'll clean up after you, like always. Don't worry Jed will sort everything out, the mug that he is.' he moaned out loud.

Jed wandered into the living room. A room that had held so many happy moments. Silence deafened him. His chest ached. Tears filled his eyes at the sight Emilia's favourite pink stuffed puppy. He traced his finger over the embroidery in the centre of a red heart on its belly, *Emilia*. He dropped to his knees, holding the pink dog to his chest. He curled up into a ball and wept. His cries echoed through the house.

His whimpers calmed into sharp sniffs that broke the silence every few minutes. He lay in a tear drenched patch on the carpet. He wiped the slime trail around his nose and mouth with the cuff of his hoodie and sat up slowly. *Come on pull yourself together, man!*

Lifting himself off the floor he wiped his face with his sleeve. Still holding the toy close to his chest, he went to search the tall cupboard for a bag. If he found anything else of Emilia's, he could collect them all together.

Taking his phone of his back pocket, he noticed the time. He had planned to meet his mum for lunch today. He couldn't face that. His head was already pounding.

JED: Hi mum, not feeling great. Can we do lunch next week? Xx

MUM: No problem. Are you ok?

When he didn't reply, she rang him. He let his voicemail deal with her for now, *I'll call her back later.*

He took himself upstairs for a shower, hoping it might wash away this nightmare. *I was just kidding myself. I was never going to be enough.*

26 – Explain Yourselves

'What the bloody hell is going on now?' Ruth screamed as she stormed through the front door.

'Wow, not even knocking now Mother? Bit rude.'

'Don't bloody start with your cheek, what's happened? I've had Jed on the phone in a right state, he said that Kara has …'

'Hi … Ruth,' Kara said in a gentle voice.

'Oh, for the love of …' Ruth held her head, 'can't make your bloody mind up between them both can you?'

'Mum!'

'Don't you Mum me. I can't believe the two of you. At it behind his back, were you?'

'It's not like that, Ruth, that's not what's happening.'

'Oh, stop I don't want to hear your excuses. The pair of you should be ashamed. After everything Jed has done for you, you just throw it all back in his face.'

'No, that's not –'

'He's absolutely broken, Kara. I've never seen him

like that before.'

'Maybe a bit like I was when I found out about my brother and my pregnant girlfriend.'

'Dan, you know it wasn't like that. You two had already broke up.'

'Oh, I see so it's one rule for one, one rule for the other. Nice.'

'Jed didn't go after her like that Dan. She needed help, and Jed was there for her.'

'And that's what I'm doing now.'

'What?'

'Mum, she's had my baby, what kind of father would I be to see them out on the streets?'

'They weren't out on the streets though, Dan. They had a home.'

'What exactly has Saint Jed told you?' Dan narrowed his eyes.

'That he came home to his neighbour telling him about a man that *she* had staying overnight. Said that he was the baby's dad, and unless she's got a longer list, that would mean it was *you*.'

'Mother!'

'I should have known you were up to something when you both disappeared from the restaurant. Why were you there?

'Mother, would you just...'

'Why would you do this to him. He's your brother!'

'MUM! Would you just... just sit down with your granddaughter. I'll go put the kettle on. Then we will talk. I think golden boy has left out a few details.'

'I'll help you.' Kara told him.

'Yes, you will want to get your story straight,' Ruth muttered.

'Mum!'

'Ok, fine. Tea would be lovely. Thank you.' Ruth said, agreeing to hold judgment until she had heard their side of the story. Ruth went to tickle Emilia who was sat quietly in her bouncer chewing her fist.

'Oh my, aren't you getting a big girl!' Ruth exclaimed, 'get them blooming handies out of your mouth, urgh dirty.'

'She's always got her fingers in her mouth. Dan thought it was because she was still hungry and gave her another bottle. Greedy little minx took it too!' Kara laughed, '... and then what happened Dan?'

'... I got slimed. All down my back, literally the whole bottle shot back out when I burped her!' Dan said screwing up his nose, 'that's why *she* finds it so bloody funny!'

He narrowed his eyes at Kara as she placed a tray of tea on the coffee table. Dan leaned over the tray and handed a cup to his mother offering her to take the handle, 'Come on Mother, it's *hot*!'

'Oh sorry, thank you Love.'

'I don't mind sacrificing a few fingerprints to play the role of your floating coaster Mother,' he joked rubbing his fingers tips together, taking his own tea and sitting in the armchair.

'Where's mine?' Kara huffed, crossing her arms dramatically.

'Right there on the table,' Dan pointed.

'You mean I have to get it myself?' Kara said throwing her hands up in the air.

'You were literally just there! You should have taken yours before you lost the use of your limbs,' Dan teased, taking a swig from his cup in torment, nearly choking as it hit the back of his throat, 'that's disgusting, I picked up the wrong mug.' He coughed, and took the cup over to Kara, 'your tea madam.'

'You've drank from it, it's probably full of your backwash now!' Kara said screwing her face as she accepted the cup from Dan.

'You're worried about my backwash? I think you've had more than my backwash in the past.'

Ruth choked on her drink, 'I don't think this is a conversation I want to hear.' She spluttered.

'Are you okay Ruth?'

'Yes, Love.' she coughed.

'I'm sorry, I don't know why he would say that.' Kara glared at Dan, who was chuckling to himself as he took his mug from the table and sat down.

'So, are you two going to tell me what happened with Jed?' Ruth asked.

Kara nodded. 'I guess I'll start,' she said.

27 – Devil in the Detail

Dan walked into the kitchen to see Kara cleaning the counter tops and swaying her hips intermittently to the radio. He smirked as he watched. She crouched down into a cupboard and pulled out cans and jars inspecting them, likely checking the expiration dates, or just be nosey. She pulled out a litre bottle of vintage whisky, holding it to the light so she could see the contents clearly, about a quarter was left in the bottle, he'd forgotten it was there. She set the bottle down and held her hands in her head.

'Dalmore Quintessence. Good stuff that, expensive, about nine hundred pound a bottle give or take, it's very nice. Not one to get leathered on. One to enjoy,' he told her.

He opened the bottle and held the top under his nose and offered it to Kara, she sniffed, the overpowering musk hit the back of her nose and made her cough.

'No?'

'*That* cost nine hundred pounds?' She said horrified.

'My dad used to drink it,' Dan explained, 'bit of a hypocrite really. He left Mum for her drinking, but he didn't mind pounding through a couple of bottles of these. Well not this exact bottle, *this* is a limited-edition, but it was a Dalmore he'd drink.'

'You don't talk much about your dad.' Kara spoke warmly.

'Not much to tell. Does this make you uncomfortable being here?' he asked, tipping the bottle as he glanced over the label.

'A little.' She confessed, 'but only because - what are you doing?' she gasped as she watched Dan pour the contents down the sink. 'Did you just pour nine-hundred-pounds worth of whisky down the sink?'

'No, that was probably only about three hundred quid of whisky I poured.'

'Why?'

'I meant what I said … it's as simple as that … what have I said now?'

'It's not you…'

'What's up then?'

'I've been getting doorbell notifications. Five in the last two minutes. Do you think I should look?'

'I take it you don't usually get so many notifications?'

'I didn't even know the app was still connected,' Kara admitted.

'If it will put your mind at ease, have a look.'

Kara opened the app and waited for it to load and muted the microphone so her voice wouldn't come through, 'what the hell is he doing?' she exclaimed.

'What?'

'Look!'

Dan screwed his up his face, 'what the *fuck* is he doing? Is he pissed?'

Kara looked at the screen, 'Oh my god. Do you think he's okay? He's banging his head against the door.'

'Definitely not, look there's that bulldog neighbour.'

'Well, at least he's helping him in.'

'Looks like he's struggling to lift him,' Dan mocked.

'He's only put him in the house. He's shut the door, look.' Kara panicked.

'I'm sure he'll be fine, he'll sleep it off and wake up with a really thick head,' Dan tried to convince her.

'He's not a drinker, what if he chokes on his own vomit or his tongue or something!'

'His tongue?'

'Please will go and check on him?'

'Me! He'll kill me!'

'What in that state? … Please?'

'Well, I've never been beaten by a drunk before … I've been beaten as a drunk -'

'Dan!'

'Alright, I'll go…'

Dan sat silent in the chair beside the bed. The soft beeping from the machine opposite brought back memories he'd sooner forget. He knew that somehow, he would be to blame for this, even though this time it wasn't his stupidity that had been at fault. He didn't force Jed to take a packet full of pills and knock then back with a bottle of Vodka, forcing his kidneys to shut down.

'Oh my God!' Ruth's broken voice cried. 'Have they given you anymore details?'

Dan shook his head.

'What happened?'

Dan shrugged, 'I'm guessing he decided to experiment in the art of cocktail making.'

'Dan.'

'Sorry Mother, but I do think I have a right to be a little ticked off, it was only a few days ago he tried taking Emmy!'

'I know, I know, but can we please just push that back a bit? Look at him!'

Dan looked at his brother laying in the bed. He had dark circles under his eyes, his skin had a yellowy tinge, and beads of sweat rolled down his forehead.

'How did you find him? I text him earlier and he didn't reply.'

'We knew he was home. Kara got a notification on her phone from that doorbell app. We saw him swaying on the front doorstep, he was banging and slurring to be let in. Then that big mouth neighbour of his appeared and helped him inside. Kara started to worry and talked me into going over to check on him. He was in a bad way. I felt for him, until he took a swing at me.'

'Oh, for God's sake. You got into a fight? And what? This is the outcome?'

'No. He stumbled, fell at my feet.'

'Liar.' Jed grumbled.

'Oh darling! You're awake!' Ruth cried, covering his face with kisses.

Jed grumbled again, 'hi, Mum.'

'I threw a punch at you.'

Dan nodded, 'and you missed.'

'You don't need to tell me. I remember.' He told Dan, who looked nervously towards his mother.

And this is where he throws me to the wolves. I've played right into his hands. Payback pending, Dan thought to himself.

Their mother perched on the side of Jed's bed and took his hand, 'Tell me what you remember.'

Jed turned slowly from Dan and looked into his mother's worried eyes. 'I was drunk, really drunk, it was so quiet. Deafening. My head was pounding. I found a packet of paracetamol. It was just paracetamol. I didn't mean to take the lot. I just wanted the pain to stop ... I just thought if I take just one more my head would stop pounding ... I went dizzy ... I fell. Then I heard a loud crash and Dan's voice. He grabbed my arm and started to pull me up ... I tried to hit him.... then nothing, it went blank. I didn't want to end up like this. I'm sorry.'

'Oh, you stupid, stupid boy!' Ruth wept, dabbing her eyes, 'and you ... why didn't you tell me, you were the one that saved him?'

'Well, that would mean me having to admit to breaking down his front door!'

'What?' grumbled Jed.

'Yeah, you're going to need a new one, sorry about that.'

28 – Message in a Bottle

'Hey, Jed buddy! What happened? I see that low life brother of yours here last night, what was he doing? Come to finish you off? Take advantage of the state you were in? I nearly came over you know, but the misses told me to keep out of it! Bloody hypocrite, she's a one to talk, the first one on the street with her nose out if any noise is raised!'

Jed squinted, 'sorry Norman, I've got a banging head, can we talk later?'

'Ah shit, yeah mate! You o'right though?'

'Everything is fine, mate, I'll get there, thanks mate.'

Jed waved off his neighbour and stepped inside his home. It was painfully silent. He wasn't convinced he would ever get used to that. It was strange, even when Kara was home, busy with the baby and didn't know he'd come into the house it never felt like this. If empty was a sound, this was it. He made his way into the kitchen and dumped his keys, phone and medication on the island by the sink. He rustled through the small drawer in front of him for his phone charger, his phone had died while he was in the hospital, *rather you than me* he joked to himself.

He left his phone on the side to charge for a few

minutes before turning it on, his mother would always scold him for doing that 'would you leave it alone, you'll ruin the battery!' she would moan at him. He waited for the screen to wake and set it down, he expected he would have a few messages of well wishes and those bloody twitter notifications. He watched his phone flash as the messages filtered in, but he wasn't expecting to see Kara's name light up amongst them.

Jed read the message again.

KARA: No one said I couldn't txt u. I had to know you were ok! Are you ok? You gave us all a scare. Pls don't do anything stupid like that again.

Searching for some hidden message within it, like *I'm sorry, let's start over, can we talk?* He couldn't make any assumptions. She didn't say it. He loved her, he always had, it hurt. After everything he had done from her and Emilia, *she's probably back with him now. I've pushed her back to him.*

If his bloody car hadn't broken down that day, he would have made it to the bar that night, none of this would have happened…

'Mate I'm Sorry, Megs is making me ask this again, she is hell bent on playing match maker. Do you remember Kara, Megan's friend?' Shane asked.

Jed chuckled, 'Yes, mate I remember you mentioning her.'

'Can Megan set you two up or what?' Shane blurted.

'Is she giving me a choice?'

'Probably, not, but ideally she just wants you to say yes.'

'So, if it goes tits up, she can't be blamed?'

'Pretty much. Mate, I'm getting hounded here, look,' Shane showed Jed the text messages from Megan, 'Can I just say you said *yes* to shut her up.'

'Yes, fine, I'll meet the girl!'

'Great, get this woman off my back!' Shane laughed, 'Megs is going to send you Kara's number. She has just said, and I quote *he must message her … well now, cos I've just told her he will*,' Shane said mimicking a feminine voice.

'Your girlfriend's a bit of a bully, mate, no offense.'

Shane agreed, 'is that her now?'

Dan looked down at his phone and smirked, 'She's even said in the message in capitals **TEXT HER NOW!** No, *Hey Jed* or nothing.'

'She's very straight to the point. Message the girl before Meg starts on me again!'

Jed saved the number to his contacts and sent a message to Kara, just as he was told to. They messaged back and forth, each asking questions for the other, light flirting.

At the end of the week, Jed received a text message from Megan, telling him to stop beating around the bush and ask Kara out. Admittedly, he found Megan slightly intimidating, so he sent the text he'd been avoiding.

They arranged to meet at a bar in town. Kara said she would sit at the bar in the corner, she often goes there to work, apparently the loud music helped her concentrate. They agreed a time and Jed signed off with **I'll see you then!** Only he didn't. His car broke down in the middle of the M6, he was travelling back from a meeting.

He text Kara with apologies, but he never received a reply. Shane never mentioned her to him after that weekend.

A while later, on one of his weekly laundry drop offs to his mum's. He found his mum running round her house excitedly with the vacuum cleaner.

'Mother?'

'Oh hello, Love! Sorry I want this place looking half decent. Dan's got a new girlfriend!'

'Oh right!'

'He's bringing her over for dinner! He's never done that before!'

'You will come, won't you? I'm doing a roast, there will be plenty!'

'Sure, what time?'

'About 6ish? I'm so excited!'

Seeing her for the first time in person, clinging on to his brother's arm offering a sweet smile and a delicate hand, 'Hi, I'm Kara.'

'Jed,' he replied smoothly, flashing a smile in return.

Her brows flickered as if her subconscious recognised him, 'it's lovely to meet you.'

She doesn't remember me, he thought to himself, 'Dan has told us so much about you.'

'He has?' she looked at Dan, who shrugged his shoulders, 'all good I hope?'

'All good,' Jed assured her.

29 – It's A Little Bit Funny

JED: Hey. Kara text me. Can u tell her I'm ok?

DAN: Can do. Good to hear.

JED: Thanks.

'Who's that?' Kara asked.

'It's Jed. He got your text, and he's okay.'

'Oh, well that's good. I'm glad he's okay.'

'When did you text him?'

'Am I not allowed to?'

'Did I say that?'

'I just wanted to know he was okay. Why did he text you?'

Dan shrugged, 'Maybe he thinks you've applied for a restraining order.'

'Don't you start.' Kara sighed.

'I wasn't.'

'Do you think you will ever work things out with him?'

'Mother will force it if anything.'

'You were close when we first met.'

'Hmm, seems roles have switched.' Dan smirked.

'Well, that was a little uncalled for.'

'Kara, we broke up, you were pregnant, you didn't tell me, then you hook up with my brother to play happy families.'

'Oh, we're doing *this* now. Can we not forget how horrible you were to me, Dan! Jed was supportive, he came to see me every day to check I was okay. When he saw I was struggling he offered his spare room. You went off with your bottled reality and left me.' Kara snivelled.

Dan waved his hands defensively, 'Alright, alright. Look I apologise. I wasn't expecting that reaction. Alright, I'm sorry. I was only joking. There's no need to bring alcohol into this.'

'It's not funny Danny.'

'I know. Can we just both agree that I'm a dick and smile?' Dan pleaded as he wiped a tear from her cheek.

'You never let me explain anything the other day.'

'Kara, please I'm sure it's very heart-warming, but I just can't listen to it, I'm not trying to be a jerk. I just can't.'

'Would you shut up and stop assuming you know everything. You don't even know what I was going to say!'

'Alright, tell me then.

'No, it doesn't matter.' Kara turned away from him.

'Well clearly it does, or you wouldn't be beetroot red right now.'

Kara felt her face, 'I'm not, am I?' she said looking into the chrome kettle.

'No, just a little rosy,' Dan teased, 'tell me.'

'I don't think I should. Everything is a mess. It's all my fault.'

'Oi, talk to me,' he ran the back of his hand down the side of her face, 'we can sort it out, whatever it is.'

'Do you think so?'

Dan didn't move his hand from her cheek. He inched closer to her to trying to gauge her thoughts. She didn't flinch, he leaned in and kissed her softly, tickling the top of her lips.

'What was that for?'

'Sorry, I ....'

'Well then I guess I'm sorry too.'

'What for?'

She pulled him towards her forcing his mouth onto hers. She ran her hand through his hair as she deepened the kiss, teasing his tongue. She pulled away from him slowly.

'What the bloody hell is going on in here.' Ruth yelled, making both Dan and Kara jump apart.

'Mother! Knock! Please!'

'Well, I apologise, I wasn't expecting to find the two of you playing tonsil tennis in the middle of the kitchen.'

'Mum, can you give us a minute, please.'

'So, you can get your story straight?'

'We're talking.'

'Oh Jesus, you're not pregnant with Jed's baby, are you?'

'Mum!'

'Okay, I'll leave you to it. No funny business! Put

the kettle on at least!'

'Alright, Mother! That woman and bloody tea!' Dan muttered.

'I'm not ... just so you know.'

'Not what?'

'Pregnant with Jed's baby.'

'That's a shame, Sally Knight would have had a field day with that one,' Dan laughed.

'Who?'

'That journalist.'

'Oh, right.'

'What did you want to tell me."

'Let me just get something first.' She disappeared momentarily and returned with a small box.

'Whoa ... hold on ... I know there's a *marry me* trend on TikTok right now but ...'

'It's not a ring, you arse.'

Dan took the box hesitantly ... 'is there a spider in here or something?'

'Would you just open it.'

He lifted the lid and removed a small purple crystal, 'what's this?'

'An amethyst.'

'It was *you*? You left me this at the hospital? I should have known!'

'I can't believe you didn't figure it out! I always have a crystal on me.'

'So, was that it? That's what you wanted to tell me? You're the *weirdo* who left the stone at the hospital? At least you didn't throw it at me. Wouldn't have blamed you if you did.'

'Do you need me to spell it out for you?'

'Please do! This is making my head hurt!'

'It's only ever been you.'

'Even after all the shit I put you through? … I-'

'Sssssh.' She placed her lips on his to quieten him.
'I let you think there was more between me and Jed … and I'm sorry.'

'What?'

'Physically, emotionally, everything.' Kara exhaled.

'Wait? You and Jed have never…'

Kara shook her head, 'I couldn't. I never wanted that relationship with him. It was just easier to let Jed assume that we were becoming a couple. He had done so much for me. And when I moved into his, we just fell into this routine, I guess. We were so comfortable with each other. To be honest part of me just wanted a little payback for how much you hurt me. Petty, I know … but nothing ever happened with Jed.'

'Oh.'

'I'm sorry I let you believe it. Sorry I let him believe it too. I feel horrible about it, I'm an awful person.'

'I take it my mum doesn't know this whole charade?'

'No. I don't think she does. Jed told me how he felt and that he wanted to put a label on things, but I just didn't know what to say without hurting him. So, I said I wasn't ready. She knows whatever Jed's told her.'

'So, you played him and led him on? Impressive.'

'Dan! I feel bad enough about it, please don't make jokes.'

'I don't get it though. You were together all the time! You want me to believe nothing happened?'

'It's true.'

'Why? You were rid of me! There was nothing stopping you.'

'Yes, there was ... You!'

'What?'

'Really? You can't figure that one out yourself?'

'No, I'm going to need you to explain it to me.'

'I love you, you idiot.'

'You do?'

'I always have. I wanted you. That's why nothing happened with Jed.'

Dan cupped her face, 'I love you too.'

'Are you two, okay? I heard shouting!' Ruth raised her voice behind the door.

'*No* Mum, were both completely naked and I've-'

Kara's mouth dropped, 'don't say that!' she gasped and slapped him on the arm.

Dan laughed as he tried to dodge her, 'ow!'

'I hope to God you're joking,' Ruth said as she pushed open the door, 'right, come on, someone tell me what's going on, please.'

'Ah, saved by the bell … I got it!' Dan looked at Kara, 'erm... I think Kara can explain this one,' and disappeared to comfort the demanding screams of little Emilia.

He heard muffled shouting while he was in Emilia's room, 'Come on Missy, let's go save Mummy from Grandma. Ooh don't tell her I called her that will you. You wouldn't want Daddy in trouble.'

The front door slammed hard, making Emilia jump as they came out of her room. Silent sobs came from the kitchen. He walked in to find Kara puffy eyed and blowing her nose into a tissue.

'What's happened? Are you alright?'

'Your mum hates me.' Kara sniffed, 'Hello baba, did you have a nice sleep,' she forced a smile for Emilia.

'She doesn't hate you. She's slammed plenty of doors in anger at me, so I wouldn't take that too much to heart.'

'I wouldn't blame her.' She sighed, rubbing the tip

of her nose with her tissue.

'Here, snuggles will make it all better,' Dan said as he placed Emilia in her arms.

'Yeah, come to Mummy,' Kara said as she stretched out welcome arms.

'Where did Mum go?'

'She's gone to see Jed.'

'Ah, of course she has. Just her nature to make sure everyone is happy. If me and Jed were football teams, she would near enough kill herself running to support one side and then the other. Can't fault her really.'

'You two are her sons, she'll love you both unconditionally, no matter what. I'm just the opposition that came along and blind tackled one of her favourite players.'

'Blind tackled?' Dan laughed.

'Oh, I don't know football analogies. All I know is she hates my guts, Jed will hate my guts and you probably hate my guts, but just don't want to admit that you do.'

'I don't hate you. Have you already forgotten our conversation? I love you. And whatever way you want to play this, I'm in.'

'Really?' Kara smiled.

'I've got no choice, have I? ... You've trapped me with a kid ...' he grinned.

'Arse.'

'So, this is us? The terrific trio?

'I hope so.'

'I just need to know the formalities so I can update my Only Fans page.'

'What?' Kara scowled.

'I'm joking, I'm joking. There's no page.'

'Daddy thinks he's funny.' Kara told Emilia, handing her back to Dan.

She walked towards the fridge, 'Should I start something for dinner?'

'No. Let's go out, I want to treat my new girlfriend.'

'Girlfriend?'

'Smooth, aren't I? No check box notes from me, babe.'

'You're an idiot.' Kara giggled.

Dan searched for a child friendly restaurant on his iPad and booked a table to a Nandos close by. They used to eat there a lot when they first started dating. He thought it might be nice to start again the same way. *What if that's a bad omen? Oh, shit.*

30 – Rip it Off

Ruth knocked abruptly on Jed's front door.

'Jesus, Mum, gently please, it's only been bodge jobbed, till I can get a new one delivered and fitted.'

'I thought Dan was paying for it?'

'He did offer to. I can pay for it myself. Can't really make him pay for it when he broke in to help me.'

'Are you going to leave me standing here like a lemon? Or are you going to invite your dear old Mother in for a coffee?'

'I don't know if I have coffee, but please old lady, come in and I'll check the cupboards.'

'How are you feeling today?'

'Like shit, but a little less like the shit I felt yesterday.' Jed smiled.

'Good.'

'What brings you here then Mother?' he asked as he looked through the cupboard, 'Oh look at that, I do have coffee.'

'I need an excuse to visit my own son?'

Jed filled the kettle and switched it on, 'no, you don't, but you don't usually try to hammer down my front door either.'

'Why did you lie to me?' she blurted out.

'About what, Mother?'

'Kara? She's told me everything.'

Jed offered a smile, 'It was real to me Mum, I wanted it to be real. I thought the more time I spent with her, eventually she would feel the same way I did.'

'Oh Jed. She's a lovely girl, she's given me a beautiful granddaughter... but was it all worth it? You lost your brother.'

'I know she wasn't mine. I scooped up a ready-made family and hoped for the best. I know how much she loves him. She wanted him back. Even if I had gone to meet her that night, before she met Dan, there's no saying that we would have worked out. I won't know that now, but my car broke down for a reason. Maybe that was fate?'

'What are you talking about?' Ruth frowned, accepting the mug of coffee Jed passed to her.

'Do you remember Shane?'

'Oh yes, Shane, lovely boy.'

Jed rolled his eyes, 'Well his girlfriend, Megan, do you remember her? They're married now.'

'No, I don't remember Megan?'

'Megan was good friends with Kara. She was trying to set me up … with her friend, Kara. Megan made me text her. We made plans to meet at a bar. My car broke down. She ended up meeting Dan. And the rest is history.'

'Oh. So, when Dan introduced her, you already knew her?'

'I recognised her when he brought her round to yours, but she was so besotted with him, she didn't blink an eyelid. When they broke up, I thought maybe I could have a chance with her ... I saw she was having a bad time, so I offered her my extra room… and I just thought, we'd spend time together and … maybe … But she still loved him. I wasn't enough, so I settled for the weird rut we ended up in.'

'Why haven't you said anything?'

'Pathetic, aren't I?'

'No Jed, you're not.' Ruth placed her coffee down and wrapped her arms around him and squeezed him close, 'You will always have me. Remember that... and when the times right you will meet someone... you can't force these things.'

'It felt real … I take it they're back together?'

'I really can't tell you that. You will have to speak to them.'

'Suppose I can't avoid them forever.'

'No. Not really.'

'Maybe I'll text Dan, arrange to go to a pub or something.'

'A pub? You two will be at each other's throats after two pints, brawling like teenagers. I don't think a bar is a good idea.'

'I was thinking more mutual grounds … but fine … no bar, we'll go for a coffee. Hopefully its better than this shit.' he pulled a face as he took another sip.

'Tastes fine to me... anyway first we need to get this place sorted. The state of it. I'll fetch you some supplies and you start cleaning that kitchen ready to cook me lunch.'

'Yes ma'am, right away, of course!'

'Enough already, get to work!' She laughed.

'Hang on a minute … me clean the kitchen? When Dan hit rock bottom, I recall you cooked *and* cleaned for him … Where's my star treatment?'

'Oh fine, I'll do it then, you sit down, relax, and don't you dare move an inch.'

'That's more like it,' Jed chuckled.

Ruth finished her coffee and left for the Co-op on the corner. She searched for the ingredients she needed to cook a fry up fit for a king. Once she was happy with everything, she made her way to the till. A selection of giant cookies caught her attention as she joined the queue, she popped one into her basket thinking it would be a nice treat for Jed.

She placed the last of her items in a bag and handed over her payment, making a mental note to tell Jed she had spent just as much on food for Dan. Her phone rang. An unknown number.

She answered hesitantly, she didn't usually answer unknown numbers, but something in her gut told her to take this one. Her everything around her started to blur. The caller kept repeating to her … *get to the hospital … An aneurism … get here quickly … next of kin … hello?* Her legs buckled and she passed out on the shop floor.

'Hey, what are you doing down there?' Ruth smiled as she poked her head under the duvet fort which he had draped over two chairs.

'Playing.'

'Ah, but what are you playing?'

He giggled at her as he presented two toy cars, 'they're racing!'

'Let's call Jed, he can be one with you?'

'He won't want to. He never wants to play with me.'

'Don't be silly, he's your brother, he *always* wants to play with you... Jed?'

'What's up?' Jed asked as he walked into Dan's bedroom.

'Come and play cars with Dan?'

'Okay, sure I'll play. Only if I can have the blue car!' he teased.

'But I want the blue car!' Dan pouted.

'Move over, idiot!' Jed nudges under the covers, grabbing hold of the blue car.

Ruth watched for a while taking it all in, listening to the clinks of metal crashing, the sudden yells of 'ow that was my finger!'

The cars skidded in all directions as the boys pushed them with all their might, racing along the laminate.

31 – When the Lights Go Out

Dan sat quietly next to his mother. Ruth stayed silent, the light in her eyes had dimmed, they were puffy and red. She slowly placed her hand in his.

'I didn't say … goodbye,' her voice trembled, 'he was fine! We were … talking, joking! … How could this happen? … why has this happened?' Tears flooded her cheeks. She rested her head on Dan's shoulder.

Dan's chest tightened. He struggled to draw in a breath as his mother sobbed into his shoulder. Her cries echoed down the silent corridor, howling like a wolf mourning her cub. He squeezed his eyes tight, reluctantly letting tears escape. He couldn't conjure any words of comfort, not without his voice breaking too. He was scared anything he said would backfire. Hoping that his silence didn't make her feel worse he listened his mother's stuttered words and held her close.

'I wish … I was there … with him … I told him … I would be right … back. I … only went to…the shop … A lady told me about her … husband, she was so … upset … he didn't have … long left … I wish you two had … sorted things out. Brothers … shouldn't fight … He wanted to make things right … with you. Oh god … I haven't called … Kara … they were close. I should … call her.' Ruth shot out of Dan's arms.

'Mum. Don't worry … I've spoken to Kara.' He placed his arm back round her shoulders.

'Oh … of course, you have … I'm sorry, Love … I just meant-.'

'Mum … it's fine … I know they were close. Jed helped her through a lot … I know.'

'When … did you call her?'

'After … you spoke with the doctor.'

'Is she … okay?'

'She's in shock … I think.'

'Are you … Okay?' Ruth asked, squeezing his hand.

'Me?' Dan took a while for the question to sink in, was he okay? It was a strange feeling. He knew his brother wasn't here, though his body was in the room behind them. He hadn't seen him yet. He wasn't sure he wanted to. If he went in there to see his brother, would he just look like he was asleep? Would he feel better seeing him? He thought about how long it had been since they bro-hugged and said *see you later, dipshit!* He wasn't ready to not have that chance again. He wanted to cling on to the only reality that kept his brother alive. They had wasted so much time.

'He text me today.'

'He did?' Ruth blubbed.

Dan nodded and showed her his phone.

JED: Dan ... Can we put all this shit behind us? Miss u bro.

'I didn't reply ... I was playing with ... Emilia ... I left it.'

'Oh Love ... You two were thick as thieves when you were younger ... My friend, Mandy, she had two boys, you won't remember, you would all play together. She was constantly having to pull those two apart. Made me feel very smug ... my two ... perfect ... boys.'

Dan smiled choking back his emotions. He needed to be here for his mother. She needed him right now. He had Kara waiting at home, they could comfort each other. His mother didn't have anything but a drawer full of photo albums. Dan cleared his throat, 'I want you to come and stay with us, Mum, for as long as you need to. I don't want you to be alone.'

Ruth smirked thinking of a response Dan had used many times before, 'So, you can keep an eye on me, make sure that I won't go near a bottle of Vodka?'

'Erm, no, Mum I didn't-'

Ruth giggled through her sniffles, 'I was joking … I would love to stay with you all and squeeze my darling granddaughter till she pops.'

'Don't squeeze her too hard, we are *quite* fond of her.'

'I guess jokes aren't my thing.'

'… and a little inappropriate Mother, *have* you been drinking?'

'Cheeky git.' Ruth sniffed.

'Excuse me, Ms Hayes?' said a man dressed in blue scrubs.

Ruth shot up to her feet, 'Yes?'

Dan did the same to offer a steady arm if she needed it.

'I'm Dr White. Would you both like to follow me?'

Dan looked to his mother, who nodded as she drew in long deep breaths. Dan felt sick, but he had to be her support. He *had* to. He closed his eyes and held his breath, puffing out his cheeks as he exhaled. Those stupid breathing techniques would never prepare him for what he was going to face. The doctor held the door open for them and they walked in together, slowly.

32 – No one Likes To Say Goodbye

Ruth stood in front of the blur of black fascinators and hats, clutching a small bottle of water and a piece of paper. The celebrant moved to the side to offer her some space as she placed the paper down onto the lectern. She took a sip from her bottle as she tried to smile at the sea of eyes staring back.

Dan leaned forward in his seat, 'Mum are you alright?' he whispered.

She nodded back at him and cleared her throat, 'I would just like to thank you all for coming today, for Jed, it warms my heart to see how many people cared for him. For those of you who don't know, my name is Ruth Hayes, I am Jed's Mother. I was lucky enough in life to be blessed with two beautiful boys. Jed, of course, and Dan, his brother. Both are amazing, and I'm extremely proud of them. They were the perfect team growing up, Jed would always take Dan under his wing, he taught him guitar. Jed was there with him every day teaching him new chords ... I have two sons ... I have two sons ...' her voice faded, and her lips trembled.

Dan got up quickly to offer her a tissue, she thanked him, insisting he went back to his seat. Kara took hold of his hand, and he sat down reluctantly.

'Sorry,' she mumbled through sniffs. 'I never told Jed how proud I was of him, but I am, and I hope he knew that. He is ... *was* ... a kind, caring person. He made me a Mother. The day I brought him home, I sat watching him sleep for hours and I knew in that moment just how special he would grow up to be. He knew what he wanted, and he went for it. He still had so much time. He still had so much he wanted to accomplish, have a family. He was amazing with my granddaughter, Emilia, so protective,' she quickly glanced over to Dan, he kissed Kara on the top of her head as she snuggled under his chin. Ruth cleared her throat, 'He has done so much for me, so much, and I've been forever grateful ... so when he turned up with a bag full of washing each week, I really couldn't say no.' She smiled softly and dabbed her face with the tissue Dan had given her, 'that's probably what I will miss the most, his cheeky smile as he strolled in with a black sack thrown over his shoulder.' She let out a small laugh as tears fell down her face, 'I know Jed wouldn't want me to cry tears for his death, he would want me to remember him with a smile ... but ... how is a mother ... supposed to say ... goodbye to her son? When that ... goodbye ... is forever? I don't want to say goodbye. So ... I'm not going to. I don't ... need to. He will always be with me ... everywhere I go. I'll get to ... see him again, so I will say, Jed ... my darling boy, I will see you soon,' she brushed off the tears that were falling down her face, kissed her hand and placed it on Jed's coffin, 'see you soon,' she whispered.

The celebrant continued with stories family members had shared with him and sent his condolences to the family, 'and finally as we say our last goodbyes to Jed preparing him for his final journey, the family have chosen a song that was one of Jed's favourites. They told me it was one he played on guitar and performed in his bedroom, later teaching it to his little brother, Dan; Summer of 69.

The wake was held in a small pub near to the family home, The White Lion. Jed had brought Dan her for his first *legal* drink when he turned 18.

'I'm going to pick Emilia up, I won't be long,' Kara said, squeezing his arm.

'On your own? Do you want me to come?'

'No, you stay. Your mother needs you here. I won't be long, it's only down the road.'

'Oh my God if one more person hangs off my shoulders baptising me with vodka, I might just have to … is that champagne?'

Dan looked down at the champagne flute in his hand and smirked, 'no Mother, it's not champagne, it's Appletiser. I had them put it in this glass so I could watch people's mouths hit the floor.'

'Please behave Dan, for today … please.'

Dan raised his hands in defence.

'What a lovely service, Ruth,'

Ruth turned to see her oldest friend and wrapped her arms around her, 'oh Jules! I can't believe it's you, it's so good to see you.'

'I just wish it was under better circumstances,' Julie replied, 'and you must be Dan.'

'I must be,' Dan smiled cheekily.

'You probably won't remember me; you were only little the last time I saw you.'

'Well, it's very nice to meet you again.'

'I'm so sorry for your loss. Both of you. From what I remember of Jed, he was a lovely boy,' Julie smiled fondly.

Dan cleared a lump in his throat, 'excuse me,' he muttered and made his way over to the far end of the bar.

'Hello, Son.'

Dan looked over his shoulder, 'you have got to be *fucking* kidding me … get the fuck out of here.' Dan spat.

Chattering around them silenced and heads turned nosily.

'What the hell is going on, I thought I said ...' Ruth's voice trailed off, '... Jay,' she spoke quietly, 'what the hell are you doing here?'

'Paying respects to *my* son,' James said coldly.

'You lost any right to call him that when you walked out on him, on them, on me,' Ruth shot her head towards the barman, 'vodka, no ice,' she barked.

'No!' Dan interjected, 'don't serve her that ... Mum what are you doing?'

'I have just lost my son, *my* son,' she glared at James, 'and I want to toast his life with a drink, that's not a crime.'

'Mum, don't. Jed wouldn't want you to do this,' Dan whispered in her ear.

Ruth gripped his hand, tears fell down her cheeks, *he's right* she thought to herself. She hadn't seen her ex-husband since their divorce hearing. He refused to have any contact with her, and that included picking the boys up from their home to spend time with them.

James cleared his throat, 'I heard about the accident, Son, I'm glad you're okay.'

Dan narrowed his eyes, 'oh, yea thanks, your "get well soon" card must have *got lost* in the post, along with birthday and Christmas cards-.'

'Son, I...'

'My name's Dan.'

James nodded, 'Alright, I'm sorry.'

'You're *sorry*?' Dan laughed, 'what the hell were you even expecting, showing up here. Did you even show up at the service?'

'I didn't think I'd be welcome.'

'But you thought you would be more welcome at the wake?'

'Daddy we're back,' Kara chirped, stopping abruptly as she studied their faces, 'is everything okay?'

Dan walked over to Kara and greeted her with a kiss on the forehead, and took Emilia from her arms, 'hello monster,' he said as he pretended to gobble her up making Emilia squeak a giggle. He placed his arm round Kara and led her towards the bar. He gave Emilia to his mother, 'safe with granny,' he told her.

'Oi!' Ruth laughed, 'we don't call Nanny that do we?'

'Kara, this is…James Hayes,' Dan narrowed his eyes.

'Oh! ... erm ... hello um, Mr Hayes.'

'Please call me James ... and who's this cutie?' he asked smiling at Emilia.

'*My* granddaughter,' Ruth told him sternly.

'She's a beauty. *Wow* I'm a Grandpa?'

'No, you're not a Grandpa, but feel free to take a good look at what you've missed out on,' Dan snarled, 'now if you don't mind, I think it's best you leave, shouldn't be too hard for you. Doors over there.'

James let out a sigh, 'for what it's worth, Son, I'm sorry.'

Dan pulled Kara into him and turned to face the bar, 'three lemonades please,' he said to the barman.

'Ruth, please can we talk?'

Ruth looked at Dan, who shrugged at her and turned away.

'The table over there, in the corner.' Ruth pointed to the far side of the pub. She gave Emilia a kiss on the cheek and gave her to Kara.

Dan grabbed her by the arm as she started to walk away, 'you don't owe him anything Mum,' he told her quietly.

'I know,' Ruth squeezed his hand, 'but he owes me.'

'We'll be right here if you need us. I'll gladly throw a punch at him if -'

'You will not!' Kara warned, 'we will stay right here. Just wave us over, if you need us,' she told Ruth as she handed her one of the lemonades Dan had just ordered.

Ruth smiled and made her way over to the table and settled down opposite her ex-husband. She held her glass on the table to hide her trembling hand, hiding the other under the table.

'I'm sorry about all that,' James told her, 'You look well, Ruth. God, I've missed out on so much.' He sighed as his eyes wandered over to Dan, Kara and Emilia.

'And who's fault is that?' Ruth snapped, taking a large gulp of lemonade.

'I didn't mean for things to end the way they did. You just made it so hard.'

'I made it hard? Oh, I'm so sorry, that you found it so bloody difficult to leave your family for some piece of meat half your age, while I picked up the slack, looked after *my* sons on my own, dealing with my own demons perching on my shoulder. Oh God I'm so sorry that was so *fucking* hard for you.' She yelled. The pub fell silent.

James cleared his throat with an awkward twitch in his smile, 'I'm sorry that came out wrong, I didn't mean-'

'Oh, shut up, no more excuses. What do you want Jay?'

'I didn't come to cause trouble. Losing Jed ... do you think Dan would give me a second chance?'

'So, you came here for Dan... not Jed?'

'You're putting words in my mouth. Of course, I came here for Jed. I don't want to lose another son.'

Ruth shook her head, 'you lost them both the day you walked out on them.'

'I'd made contact with Jed a few months ago, found him on Facebook.'

'Right,' Ruth snorted.

'I want to make things up to Dan.'

'Do you? Well ... He's on the socials too you know. Trended a few times lately, but you would know that. Probably the reason you're here! Good luck with that,' Ruth said as she got up from her seat.

'Ruth, wait. I am sorry. For what I did, leaving. For what it's worth. You look amazing. You really do.'

'Yes, I do. Goodbye James,' Ruth forced a smile through the pain in her chest as she walked back towards the bar.

'Are you alright Mum?' Dan asked.

'I will be, love. I will be.'

33 – Writing Again

Kara knocked lightly on the door to the room Dan had enclosed himself in for the past week, 'Dan?' she said peeping her head round the door.

'Hey,' Dan smiled at her.

'Hey yourself. You've hardly left this room since the funeral. Are you okay?'

'I'm alright. Don't hide behind that door. Come here I want to show you something.'

'Show me what?'

'This,' he pointed to the computer screen, 'now I want your honest opinion,' Dan grinned.

'Honest opinion?' Kara repeated frowning at his laptop, 'what have you been up to?'

'Listen.'

Dan tapped the small triangle by a load of what looked like squiggles and she listened to the gentle strumming of a guitar. She gasped when she heard the voice, 'that's you! Oh my god! You made this?'

'Would you please listen?'

Kara rolled her eyes and listened to the story Dan was telling on the recording, her eyes glistened as she smiled through the song, 'this is what you have been doing up here? You're writing again?'

'What do you think?' he asked as the playback stopped.

'It amazing. It's so good to hear your voice again.'

'Do you have another?'

'I do, but you can't hear it ... yet.'

'Why not?' Kara pouted.

Dan smirked at her, 'because you can't.

'So, you've got me in here to tease me. Well, that's just charming, anyway, dinners nearly ready, and your mum will be here soon,' Kara checked her watch, 'so get that cute bottom of yours down those stairs, Hayes.'

'Alright. I'll just finish this up and I'll be down.'

'Are you going to let your mum listen to any of these?'

'Not today. I wanted to see how you'd react first.'

'What do you mean?'

Dan pushed himself up from his desk chair and cupped her face, 'I don't want this to make you feel ... I know I was a dick back then and ...'

Kara placed her fingers over his mouth and shushed him, 'If this is what you want to do, I'll support you. Don't let the past drag you down. I'm here, I'm staying. Besides, you step a toe out of line, and I'll set Emilia on you,' Kara joked and gave him a quick kiss.

Dan chuckled, 'she'll keep me in check. Where is my little sidekick?'

'Asleep in her pushchair.'

'Why is she in her pushchair?'

'We've been to the Co-op, ten minutes in that thing and she's out for the count.' Kara turned her head towards the sound of a muffled cry, barely muttering the word "Mama".

'It's awake,' Dan gasped, 'It's like she knows we're talking about her.'

Kara laughed and made her way down the stairs.

'Hello, sleepy head. Are you ready for din-dins?' Kara said as she scooped her up, 'are we going to show Nanny how you can push your walker?'

The door knocked, 'Hey Nanny!' Kara squeaked.

'Na-na-na,' dribbled Emilia.

'Hello gorgeous girl. Hi Kara, love,' Ruth smiled, and she greeted her with a peck on the cheek.

'Hello, Mother!' Dan shouted as he made his way down the stairs.

'Dan,' Ruth greeted him, 'are you okay, Love? Kara told me earlier she had hardly seen you.'

Dan narrowed his eyes at Kara who quickly excused herself to check on the chicken, placing Emilia in her play pen on the way.

'I'm fine Mum. I'm good,'

'Are you sure? What have you been doing?'

'Working.'

'Working?' Ruth repeated.

'Yes! Working! Why is that so hard to believe?' Dan raised his voice.

'There's no need for that tone Mr Bigshot, it was just ... unexpected that's all.'

'Sorry, I didn't mean to sound so aggressive, I'm

nervous.'

'Nervous?' Ruth and Kara said in unison.

Dan bounced his eyes between them, 'I think you two have been spending too much time together.'

'Stop deflecting and tell us,' Ruth demanded.

'I booked a gig,' Dan shrugged.

Ruth stared at him in disbelief. 'Did you know about this?' she asked a stunned Kara, who could only manage to shake her head.

'Don't freak out, it's only a pub gig. In memory of Jed.'

Ruth's eyes watered almost immediately, 'Oh Dan.'

'And before anyone says anything, it's not a paid gig, well not in the sense of me getting any benefit from it. It's for charity, one that helps other families through loss and what we've been through. I've left the landlord to decide which one would be best ... why are you looking at me like that?'

Ruth flung her arms around Dan and gripped him tight, 'what an amazing thing to do.' She wept.

'Mother ... Can't breathe,' Dan wheezed.

'Oh, I'm sorry,' she said, releasing him slowly, 'I am so proud of you.'

'Don't gush at me just yet Mother, it could all be one big disaster.'

'I doubt that You will be amazing.' Ruth praised.

'So that's what the new music is for?' Kara asked.

Dan nodded, 'I'll do some old stuff too.'

'Oh my God I can't wait to see you back on a stage,' Kara squealed.

'I'd hardly call their beer-stained wooden flooring a stage,' Dan laughed.

'It's a start,' Kara cheered as she pulled the chicken out of the oven, 'Oh my God this smells amazing! Ready for dinner?'

34 – Starting Over

Dan had been at The White Lion most of the afternoon to set up. He was only playing a guitar and arrived far too early. Nerves were starting to kick in as he agonised over whether his guitar was tuned properly. He fiddled with the speakers, testing them more times than he needed to, making the barmaid jump and drop a glass to the floor.

'Shit. Sorry!' *Too loud,* he thought to himself as he turned down the output volume again. It was a long time since he played in such a small venue, or any venue for that.

'Dan, would you like a drink?' the landlord, Bryan asked from behind the bar.

'Please, a diet coke would go down quite nicely,' Dan replied reaching into his back pocket for his wallet, *a shot of whiskey would go down better,* a tiny demon surfaced with a nudge. Dan shook him off and took out a £10 note.

'No, no this one's on me, mate. You put that away,' Bryan said shaking his head, 'come and take a seat, take five,' Bryan chuckled.

Dan sat on a small stool around the table Bryan had sat at, 'cheers for the drink, bud,' Dan said as he chugged down half a glass.

'No problem looks like you needed it. So, the plan for this evening, we're going to have a donation bucket on the bar, by the till so we can keep an eye on it, and another will be floating around the punters. The barmaids will take it out every so often. Your mum's been kind enough to give us pictures of Jed, which we will place around the bar area, I think Dot's planning on putting together a collage thing, I dunno what she said,' Bryan laughed, 'she loves all that stuff, my wife.'

Dan smiled, taking another gulp of his coke.

'Oh, and the charity have been helpful, they sent over some posters we can put up, just so people know where their money's going. Are you alright mate you're very quiet, I thought you'd be used to a lot more than this being a big shot celebrity.'

Dan cleared his throat, 'it's been a long time.'

'Ah you'll be fine once you're up there. He was a good lad, your brother. I know you had a bit of a tough time with each other, but what family doesn't. You'll do Jed proud mate.'

'I appreciate you saying that. Thanks, bud.'

'We also thought about having a karaoke session after your set. Not using your equipment, obviously, we have a karaoke machine in the back there. The punters get quite competitive. It's a good laugh, would give you a chance to enjoy yourself with your family.'

'Sounds great,' Dan grinned as he imagined his mum belting out a Madonna number, perfect for those who were hard of hearing. She loved a karaoke, but that was a long time ago and fuelled by a few shots of vodka.

'Right, we best get this show on the road, only a couple of hours to go!' Bryan announced rubbing his hands together, he was confident Dan was going to bring in a crowd.

Kara had put an announcement on twitter and Facebook, but Dan didn't dare open his accounts to see the responses, even when Kara had told him a lot of them were positive. *I'm doing this for Jed, not me* he reminded himself, although it didn't do much for his nerves, *The pressure is on.*

Dot led Dan out to the kitchen, referring to it as his "backstage area". She offered him a burger, and a piece of rich chocolate cake, which he refused surprising even himself. He accepted a glass of water and a packet of ready salted crisps which Dot insisted he ate before going "out to his adoring fans" he thanked her, promising he'd eat them.

'So, here's where you're hiding?' Kara teased, 'what time are you starting?'

'In about half hour,' Dan replied as he glanced at his watch, 'where's Emmy?'

'She's out there with your mum, she insisted we had the best seats in the house,' she chuckled, 'Bryan reserved us a table.'

'Good of him, but I doubt it was needed.'

'Why?'

'Not really *well known* anymore, am I?'

'There are plenty of talented musicians that just play at their local boozer. You don't need to headline Wembley to be amazing.' She said and kissed him softly, 'why don't you come out for a drink before you go on?'

'Well, I suppose it would be less of a blow walking out to the tumble weeds now,' he joked.

'Dan I'm not kidding, there are *a lot* of people out there, I literally had to force my way through to get here.'

'You know it's really not nice to play with me like that, I'm really starting to regret saying yes to this.' Dan stood still taking in deep breaths.

'Are you okay? I've never seen you like this before.'

'Well, if it's not that obvious, I'm absolutely bricking it. I don't want to let anyone down.'

'You won't. I won't let you,' she smirked and nudged him in the side.

Dan pulled her into him, 'I love you,' he gushed tickling her nose with his, he kissed her just as she was about to speak, which made her giggle into his mouth.

'Come on *Mr Celeb*, let's get you through that sea of hardcore fan girls.'

'Really? There are girls?' Dan grinned cheekily, shoving Kara playfully aside.

Kara slapped him on the chest and pulled him through the sliding door into the pub. Dan was greeted by loud cheers and people chanting his name. He couldn't believe it, the pub had far exceeded its capacity. Dan's jaw almost hit the ground he shook random hands and high fived Bryan's grandson as Kara steered him around them. People were kind enough to make as much space as they could so they could pass through. As they reached their table Dan sat heavily on a chair, 'What the fuck? … why is there … how … does Bryan have a licence for this many people?'

'GREAT TURNOUT!' Bryan yelled at Dan from behind the bar, sliding a glass of coke over to him, 'We're gonna make a killin'! Let's just hope the police don't shut us down!'

Dan nodded a thank you for the drink and turned to Emilia who was pulling at the sleeve of his shirt for his attention, she beamed a gappy toothed smile at him and stretched out her arms, 'da-da-da-da!'

'Hello, my darling girl, have you come to wish Daddy luck?'

Emilia squealed, kicked her legs and pulled herself to her feet by clutching at the front of his shirt, then popped her head over his shoulder so she could see everyone behind him. She squeaked, *'Hiya!'* at a few people who cooed at her, she shied away into Dan's lap, slapping her hands on his chest.

'Oi, bully!'

'Dan, mate you might wanna think about jumping on, there's people lining up round the block to get a glimpse of you, no joke!'

Dan's eyes almost popped out of his head, he turned to Kara, and mouthed, 'what the fuck is going on?'

'Come on big-shot don't want to keep these tumbleweeds waiting,' Kara teased.

Dan narrowed his eyes as her. He passed Emilia over to his mother and slowly made his way over to the barstool Bryan placed in front of his microphone stand.

Dan took in a deep breath.

He threw his guitar strap over his head.

Looked towards the sea of eyes.

And switched on his mic.

'Hey everyone, thank you-' he stopped abruptly as his speakers hissed over his words, 'sorry!' he raised his hands, 'there that should be better. Alright.'

Dan took in another breath.

'As I was saying, thank you everyone for coming tonight. For those who don't know me, my name is Dan Hayes,'

A few "wooos" came over the crowd. The loudest of them was Kara.

Dan giggled into the mic, 'I'm here this evening in memory of my late brother, Jed. There are charity donation buckets around, if you can help contribute to a great cause it will help families who have also suffered a heart-breaking loss, the same as we have. As much or as little as you can give will be greatly appreciated. I've been working on some new songs which I'm going to play for you all tonight and then good old Bryan's going to bring it home with the Karaoke machine, so I'm just the warmup act for you guys,'

Dan started to tease a few chords together on his guitar as he spoke, 'so this first song is one I've written recently while I was sat in Starbucks wondering why I was alone. It's called, *why did you go?* Hope you like it.'

As he strummed the last chord the room erupted with cheers, and woops, with a standing ovation from Kara and Ruth. Emilia screamed and slapped her chubby hands together.

'Thank you,' he bowed his head, and took a gulp of water that Bryan left on a small table to his side, 'now I promised I wouldn't make this night about me, but I couldn't not dedicate this next song to the absolute love of my life, Kara,' he smiled in her direction and watched her blush. Her eyes were already welling, 'well it's all about her, so I'd be in serious trouble if I didn't dedicate it to her. This one's for you, babe.'

Kara listened intently, watery eyed. The story of their up and down romance; "the good, the bad and the ugly" as he so lovingly named it. He sang every word to her, not once looking away. He told her how grateful he was to have her in his life and what he hoped for their future. Kara couldn't stop her tears falling. She wiped her face with the back of her hands and threw herself at him on his final chord, knocking him off his stool.

The speakers hissed at the disruption, 'maybe that

should have been my final song? ... are you alright?' he asked Kara as her sniffs echoed into the mic.

Kara composed herself, kissed him on the cheek and returned to her seat, still wiping her eyes.

'That *was* her by the way,' he joked to the crowd, which most found amusing.

Dan continued to play a few songs from his past, which, to his surprise, people were singing along to. Just for fun he decided to throw the mic in front of random people to finish off the lines for him. A few shrieked at him, stunning them to silence.

'I've saved the most important song for the very end. The reason we're all here tonight. This song is for *you* Brother,' he flashed a smile as he began playing the emotional melody, 'hopefully he can hear this, wherever he is.' he said looking above.

He sang about their close bond as children, his brother took him under his wing and when they went their separate ways, he wished he could take things back, repair their brothers' bond. Dan glanced over to his mother who was choking on her tears, which nearly broke his voice. He powered through giving an emotional finish.

A thunderous applause erupted.

'Thank you very much. Wow, this has been an

emotional rollercoaster tonight. I think you have heard enough from me, it's your turn now. Bring out the karaoke, Bryan!'

'More! One more!' someone shouted from the back.

'Can we get pictures?' Someone else called out.

Bryan made his way over to Dan and pull him into a one-armed hug, 'Well done mate, well done,' he said patting him on the shoulder, 'Okay everyone, give me a minute to set this up ...'

'We want pictures!'

'Pictures?' Bryan repeated, looking over to Dan.

Dan shrugged, 'I don't mind doing a few selfies.'

'Alright, for selfies, we need a donation, doesn't matter how much as long as you give something!' Bryan yelled out and looked over to Dan to check that was okay, Dan gave him a thumbs up. 'Our lovely Sandy, will hold out the donation bucket, if you form a queue for selfies just along the bar, alright? Great!' Bryan said as he turned his attention to the karaoke machine. He moved Dan's equipment into the corner.

Dan stood by the end of the bar with a permanent smile, taking selfies with those that wanted them. He thanked people for their heart-warming comments, for coming out and, most importantly, for donating.

Bryan announced the karaoke machine officially up and running and invited the first duet of the night to claim the mics, as Dan snapped his last selfie. Sandy took the donation bucket behind the bar and went on to serve customers crowding the beer pumps.

'Oh, Dan you were amazing,' Ruth praised. She leaned over to kiss his cheek before he sat done next to Kara.

'Yeah, nicely done, Hayes,' Kara winked and offered her cheek, 'that song was beautiful, even better than the one *all* one about me.'

Dan squeezed her hand and guided it up to his lips, 'So this little one didn't quite make it through, eh?' Dan chuckled, staring fondly at his daughter.

'Oh, she tried. She really did, the milk was her kryptonite. She fell fast asleep as soon as she drank it,' Kara smiled, 'bless her, she loved what she stayed awake for.'

'I don't understand how she can sleep through all this noise?'

'Should probably get her home soon though,' Kara told Dan, 'You stay though, seriously, enjoy it. You both deserve to.'

'Don't be silly, I'm too old for all this, I'll take Emilia and you both stay,' Ruth insisted.

'No, honestly, it's fine. This is for your son, and your brother, its only right that you both be here ... and if I'm honest, I'm dying for a cup of tea! So, you two stay and I'll see you both back home.' She told them, planting a kiss on Dan's lips.

'Kara, are you sure love?'

'Of course, I am.'

'Well, if you insist, I stay out and party all night, who am I to argue?' Dan quipped, 'But what kind of gentleman would I be if I let you walk to the car on your own? Come on, I'll help you with Emmy.'

35 – Back in Business

'What a crazy night!' Bryan exclaimed, 'I can't believe how many people turned up, the tills are overflowing! We've raised a decent amount too; those buckets are heavy! Well done, lad. Well done,' Bryan praised slapping Dan on the back.

'That was definitely down to your karaoke machine,' Dan replied as he sipped back his coffee. Dot had kindly gone out to the back kitchen to make him one, he'd had his fill of Coke. she was insisting he had a drink to celebrate.

'Thank you both for doing all this,' Ruth expressed to Bryan and Dot, holding her glass of Orange up to toast them, their glasses met with a clink, 'Dan bring your cup in!'

Dan did as he was asked and lifted his cup, 'cheers guys, and thank you!'

'We should have you perform here again,' Bryan winked at Dan, 'what do you think?'

Dan smiled, 'I really enjoyed tonight, I must admit.'

'Settled then, we'll have a look at the calendar and work something out, but this one your being paid for!'

Dan tilted his head in appreciation and took another gulp of coffee. He noticed his phone vibrating in his pocket, he pulled it out to see a message from Kara screaming at him.

KARA: OMG!! UR TRENDING ON TWITTER!!! XX

Dan frowned at the message, and loaded up his twitter account...

'Holy shit!' he shouted.

'What? What's wrong?' Ruth asked with a worrying shake in her voice.

Dan whipped his phone round, flashing the screen at her, 'People have been sharing videos from tonight!'

'Oh, Wow! How do you feel about that?'

'I dunno,' he shrugged, 'weird ... a good weird ... and just a bit concerned about what the comments might say.'

'Fuck the haters, isn't that what the kids say these days?'

'Mother, language!' Dan exclaimed, 'Gran would roll in her grave!'

Ruth giggled and shrugged.

Dan turned to Bryan and Dot, as he out his phone back into his pocket, thank you for tonight, it's been a great experience, really enjoyed it, but I best get back home.'

'Yes, we should,' Ruth agreed, 'do you need any help tidying up before we go?'

'No, don't be daft. The cleaners will sort this tip out in the morning, we'll be going straight to bed I think,' Bryan yawned, 'you guys get off. You've been brilliant tonight, Dan, thank you. Done your brother proud.'

Kara was still awake when they got back, Ruth excused herself and made her way to the guest room she had claimed, to change into her comfys.

'I'll be back down for a cuppa, get the kettle on,' Ruth instructed Dan.

'Did you read any of the comments?' Kara asked, jumping up as Dan walked towards the kettle.

'Nope.' Dan stated, 'I take it, you did though. I don't want to know if they are bad.'

'But they aren't, there's a lot of positive stuff, like *"OMG! That can't be the same guy, he sounds amazing!"* and *"wow, what a difference!" "OMG where was he playing? Can't believe I missed this!"* ooh I love this one, *"I knew he had it in him!"* See positive,' Kara smiled.

'Positive ... ish,' Dan smirked, 'sounds more like they question my ability.'

'... and that's not a good thing?' Kara frowned, 'you've proved them wrong.'

'There will still be some really shitty comments in between those.'

'Well, you can't please everyone,' Kara shrugged, 'are you making tea?'

'Yes, as per Mother's instructions, you want one?'

'Might as well.'

Dan pulled another mug from the cupboard.

'So, how many girls threw themselves at you?'

'What?' Dan huffed, 'no one threw themselves at me!'

'Calm down, I was only messing with you. How long did it take for Bryan and Dot to get all everyone out?'

'A lot of them pretty much disbursed after having their photo, was only really the locals and a few other groups that stayed for the karaoke, still busy even then, but at least you could move,' Dan explained, 'Mum pulled though,' he added as he spotted her coming through the doorway.

'What?!'

'I did not, cheeky bugger,' Ruth fumed.

'Tea Ma'am,' Dan announced as he placed a mug in front of her.

'Did Emmy settle when you got back?' Dan asked Kara as he gave her a mug.

'She was fine, fussed a bit when I changed her into PJs, but she went back off, no problems. So relieved, I had visions of chasing her round the front room.'

'Have you told Kara what Bryan said?' Ruth interjected.

'No, *Mother*, I haven't, give me a chance!'

'Well? What did he say?' Kara asked eagerly.

'He wants me to do another set, a paid one this time.'

'That's brilliant!' Kara cheered.

'I bring in a decent crowd,' Dan bragged.

'Has he said when?'

'They're going to look at the calendar.'

'Just don't let that alter ego of yours ruin it,' Ruth

warned.

'Mother!' Dan yelped, 'I won't fuck up, I promise, got too much to lose, this time,' he draped his arm over Kara's shoulders.

'Finally, you release I'm a catch!' Kara joked.

Dan pulled a face, and sucked in air through his teeth, 'oh, wow, this is awkward ... I was talking about Emmy.'

'Well, she is the most important one, so I'll let you off ... arsehole,' she laughed nudging into him.

Dan turned her face to look at him and leaned to kiss her.

'Oh, for god's sake, you two, if all its going to be is public displays of affection ...'

'Calm down Mother it's just a kiss, I haven't thrown her over the counter.'

Ruth covered her face and shook her head, 'Right, on that note, I think I'll call it a night.'

'Wait Mum, I want you to stay a minute to see something.'

'I don't want to witness you canoodling on the counter, thank you.' Ruth snubbed.

'Mother, please get your mind out of the gutter.'

Dan wandered over to the corner cupboard. He opened it and pulled out a small box. Dan smiled widely, 'Kara, my life started with you, alright I admit I had a funny way of showing it in the past, but I hope I've made it up to you since then, and if I haven't ... well ... then I want to spend the rest of my life trying to. You have quite literally been my rock through everything, and I don't want to be without you. Whatever journey life takes us on, I only want to share it with you.'

Kara's eyes welled, and her brows burrowed as he opened the box, 'Dan that's a tumble stone, I gave that to you.'

'What?' Dan looked confused, 'shit, wrong box!' he panicked, darting back over to the corner cupboard.

'Wait, there's ... this isn't a joke?' Kara stammered.

'No, it's not a joke, I just pulled the wrong bloody box out ... ah ha! Got you ya ... bastard! ... Let's try that again,' he beamed as he opened the box, presenting a white gold princess cut trilogy ring, two diamonds glistened either side of a sparkling purple stone, 'You gave me the idea for the centre stone, all I need is you, and with you wearing amethyst, well it's just another reason to keep you close. Kara, will you marry me?'

Kara struggled to hold back her tears and just nodded, finally managing a silent squeak of the word *yes*. She swung her arms round his neck, squeezing him tightly as she buried herself into his shoulder.

'Oh my god, my boy! Oh, I'm so happy for you both!' Ruth wailed, 'we need champagne!'

'Yes, that's *just* what we need! Where is your head Mother?' Dan shook his head.

'Sorry, you're right, *normal* people get to celebrate with champagne … let's see what you have and whatever it is we're drinking from champagne flutes!' she insisted as she rummaged through the fridge, 'Ah! Shloer, white grape … perfect substitute! Now where are those flutes?'

'I'll get them!' Dan said turning to the cupboard behind and taking out three glasses. He placed them on the counter.

Ruth skipped over with her champagne substitute, filled the glasses, and passed a glass each to Dan and Kara.

'Thank you, Mother,'

'Thank you,' Kara blushed admiring the sparkle on her finger.

Ruth raised her glass, 'to the future, whatever adventures it holds. Congratulations my darlings!'

'To the future,' said Dan and Kara in unison and joined their glasses with a delicate clink.

Dan watched contently as his mother inspected the ring on Kara's hand. He absorbed the expressions on their faces, the glimmer in their eyes. *He* had done that; *he* was responsible for their happiness. That was his focus, and with *her* by his side anything was possible, *we'll be just fine.*

36 – Emilia

'Hey, what are you watching?' Kara asked Dan as she settled in the seat next to him.

'Emmys... nothing else really worth watching.'

'And this is?'

'I like to show my support … now I finally have one.'

'Have what?'

'An Emmy! … Dur!' Dan replied with a rolled eye.

'You don't have an Emmy!' Kara giggled.

'I do too!'

'Show me then, prove it.'

'Alright, I will ... but what you have got to understand is … I wasn't given this *Emmy* in the *traditional* way-'

'You didn't steal it, did you?'

'No, *I* didn't steal the *Emmy*… I wasn't even given it to hold, and I was there on the night. The *Emmy* was accepted on my behalf … shall we say.' Dan smirked.

'Right ... but you were there?'

'I was indeed.'

'So where is this award hidden then?' Kara asked, looking round the room.

Dan smiled as he called through to Emilia playing in the other room.

Emilia came thundering towards Dan in her princess heels that were four sizes too big, holding a toy guitar, 'Look, Daddy!'

'Oh wow, you look beautiful, a rocking Princess, I like it,' he beamed as she stood clonking her heels on the wooden floor, 'come here a second.'

Emilia clattered over with a smile and Dan scooped her up into his arms, both shoes and the toy guitar crashed loudly to the floor making Emilia shriek.

'Shush!' Kara giggled you'll wake your brother!'

Emilia shot her hands up to cover her mouth.

'Sorry, that's my fault! Naughty daddy! I didn't realise Jed was still sleeping.'

Kara exhaled loudly, 'so you were telling me about this Emmy?'

'This … is my *Emmy*,' Dan boasted as he held Emilia up in the air.

'Daddy, put me down!' Emilia snorted trying her best not to wake her brother.

'Oh, I knew you were having me on...' Kara huffed.

'It's the circle of life …' Dan sang loudly, lifting Emilia up higher.

'Oh, for God's sake.' Kara laughed.

'What? We love a Disney film, don't we?' He said as he belted out the next few lines, 'come on Emmy, join in,' Dan said as he mumbled the words he didn't know, with Emilia giggling the whole while.

The Ego Effect

Creative Hats

Acknowledgements

Some can only dream what it would be like to be a successful artist taking over the charts with an infectious melody. During my teenage years, I had that dream. My closest friends, Sabrina and Lakesha, and myself formed a group called Esenel. We even registered our group name on a band site and were able to print off our "official" certificate, not sure how legitimate that was. We were three daydreamers with stars in our eyes. We would write our own songs, just the words, our attempts trying to add the backing music sadly failed. Most of the songs we recorded ourselves ... acapella, and I pray those cassette tapes never see the light of day again!

One song has been an intermittent earworm over the years. A song which I have fondly mentioned in this book. Why Did You Go was written by the wonderful Sabrina. Thank you, Sabz for letting me to use some of the words we once sang together in my garage all those years ago.

My nanna and grandad, Bryan and Dot, ran a pub called The White Lion when I was younger. I gifted my landlord/lady characters their names in their memory, this way they are kind of taking this journey with me. My nanna loved reading, and I'm sure she would have been the first to read this cover to cover.

My husband's amazing God Mother, Pat, was kind enough to read through my final draft. I must admit, I was very nervous awaiting her review, but being the super reader she is, I didn't have to wait too long! Thank you so much Pat for your kind words, and for giving my confidence a little boost.

Special thanks to my mentor … editor … friend, Kelly, at Creative hats, without whom, none of this would be possible. Kelly has been one of my biggest supporters since joining one of her writing classes. Her enthusiasm and encouragement has pushed me throughout the years I've known her. This book has been quite a while in the making and Kelly has read, re-read, and edited and never grumbled when I've chirped … 'oh I've added a few extra words …' Thank you for everything, Kelly.

To my husband, my walking thesaurus, thank you for all your praise, your patience, and for convincing me not to give up. You always believe in me, even when I don't believe in myself.

Finally, to my family and friends, there are far too many to mention individually. I just want to say thank you for supporting me in every way, it means the world. You know who you are.

Nicola x

Nicola Warner

Nicola grew up in Hitchin, Hertfordshire. As a child she loved music, dancing and creating stories. Today she lives in her hometown with her husband, their two children, and their dog. In her spare time, she runs a gemstone jewellery business, carries out marketing promotion for other authors, binges Netflix (just for story inspiration, of course!) and reads widely.

Nicola has several published collaboration books in her name and created the group, 'Fantastic Writers' to support up and coming authors.

This is her first solo novel.

She only officially began writing in 2020, after joining local writing groups to gain the confidence she needed to finally put her ideas to paper.

Nicola is currently working on her next Novel to be published late 2023.

You can contact Nicola via the following handles – she would love to hear from you:

Instagram: nicolawarnerauthor

Twitter: @pixie_nicsi

Printed in Great Britain
by Amazon